"That's what has stumped the detectives working these cases," Robin said. "The women have no memory at all on the day they were taken."

"Any record of some of them being hypnotized to bring up lost memories?" Sarge asked.

"Six of them that I can tell tried that," Robin said. "I'm still digging, but what the pattern is that the women seem to remember is leaving for an errand on their own, then waking up as they are being married to a tall man wearing a plastic face in some sort of wedding chapel. They are drugged and can't speak or even talk. Then they are taken to a nearby bedroom and raped, then the next thing they remember, they are in their cars."

"Drugs," Sarge said a moment before Pickett could.

"That's the theory on this," Robin said, "but no drugs were found in the women's systems in any fashion. No DNA traces, nothing."

"So we have someone who knows chemicals and drugs," Pickett said.

"You said they were married?" Sarge asked Robin. "Someone else there?"

"Yes," Robin said. "A third person was always involved in the ceremony wearing an Elvis mask and dressed like Elvis."

# ALSO BY DEAN WESLEY SMITH

# DEAD HAND

A Cold Poker Gang Mystery

## DEAN WESLEY SMITH

**Dead Hand**

First published in a different form in *Smith's Monthly* #29, February 2016
Published by WMG Publishing
Cover and Layout copyright © 2021 by WMG Publishing
Cover design by Allyson Longueira/WMG Publishing
Cover art copyright © pilotL39/Depositphotos
ISBN-13: 978-1-56146-490-6
ISBN-10: 1-56146-490-2

# DEAD HAND

### Dead Hand:

*In poker any hand that has been eliminated from the action because of a problem with the hand, the betting, or some other infraction. It can also mean a hand that is clearly beat at the end of round, but the player played it anyway.*

# A WEDDING DRESS

# PROLOGUE

*May 17th, 2010*
*Las Vegas, Nevada*

Trudy Patterson ran her hand along the lace edge of her white wedding dress as it hung in her suite's bedroom. The dress was so beautiful, with a full skirt and short train, and it fit her perfectly, almost magically, especially over her shoulders.

She had hung it out in the open just to be able to stare at it the last few days and enjoy the wonderful future it promised. Amazing how a simple dress could mean so much.

Outside Trudy's top floor suite, the sun was shining and the day was promising to be warm. She had some errands to run, then she would pick up Tommy, the love of her life, at the airport and they would have dinner. So when she got back from the errands, she needed to put the dress away so he wouldn't see it. That would be bad luck.

She didn't really believe in that sort of thing, but when it came to getting married, she was going to take no chances.

3

But for the moment, she liked having the wonderful dress and all it offered for a future out in the open.

The dress had been her grandmother's on her father's side. Her grandmother would have been proud to see Trudy wearing it, but her grandmother had died a year before Trudy met Tommy in their last years of college.

Tommy's parents and family and friends would arrive tomorrow from Los Angeles and Trudy's parents and sister would fly in the following day.

In three days, Trudy would walk down the aisle in that dress in a beautiful chapel in the rocks just outside of town and marry Tommy. They had been living together now in Denver for three years and both of them had always wanted to get married in Las Vegas. Now, it was finally going to happen, just as they had both dreamed and planned.

She had been here for almost a week, arranging all the details for the rehearsal dinner, the wedding, the justice of the peace, the flowers, everything. Her mother had offered to get time off work and come and help her, but Trudy had wanted to do it alone. She felt that would make it even more special.

Her hand brushed the dress again, then she checked herself in the bathroom mirror to make sure her long brown hair was still tied back and her shorts weren't riding up on her and her light blue blouse was buttoned correctly.

All fine. Just three last quick errands, not more than a few hours, and she would come back, shower, and change to meet Tommy.

She took her rental car keys, her small brown purse, and a bottle of water and headed out of the suite's door.

The hotel's security cameras followed her to the valet parking, where she got in her blue 2010 Ford Taurus rental car, buckled her seat belt, and pulled into traffic without a problem.

She was never seen alive again.

Five days after she was scheduled to be married and her frantic family and fiancé shouted at everyone they could shout at to get help, Trudy Patterson's body was found in a white wedding dress, holding a bouquet of red, wilted flowers, sitting in her rental car, parked at the top of a slight ridge looking out over Las Vegas.

Because she had been sitting in the hot car with the windows up for three days before being found, cause of death was never determined.

And with her fiancé and family all having complete alibis, there were no suspects.

None.

Within months, her case went cold and her grandmother's wedding dress, the one that had hung in the suite, not the one she wore in death, was put back in a box for storage.

# CHAPTER ONE

*October 18th, 2016*
*Las Vegas, Nevada*

Retired Las Vegas Detective Debra Pickett locked her silver Jeep Grand Cherokee SUV on the second floor of the Golden Nugget parking garage and then, out of years of habit, checked everything around her as she started for the sky bridge.

She walked with a long stride for her five-four size. Not quick, like would be expected, just long, which allowed her to cover more ground. At sixty-one years old, she kept her hair short and dyed her natural brown, the color it had been before it started turning gray.

Her color of gray had been faded and ugly, not silver like her mother's had been. So keeping it brown was her only choice.

Many a person over the years had underestimated her thin, wiry stature and paid a price by often ending up face down on the pavement. She had a reputation around the station of being too tough to mess with and she liked that. She had played it up at times to her advantage.

Around her, the four-story concrete parking garage was mostly quiet. A young couple headed for their car on the far side, her heels clicking on the pavement and her far-too-short mini-skirt hiking up even as she tried to keep it down. A black Ford with another couple cruised upward along the ramp looking for a place to park, its engine surprisingly silent.

At ten in the evening, the air was starting to have a slight bite to it. She loved this time of the year in Las Vegas. Comfortable days, cool nights. Perfect.

She was dressed in her normal jeans, a light-colored tan blouse, and a light-tan cloth jacket. She had her badge in her back pocket and her gun in her large purse. She normally liked to carry the gun in a holster under a jacket, but wearing a gun while playing cards at Lott and Julia's place just felt odd.

The noise from the bands over on the Fremont Street Experience was faint in the garage. It was still too early for most people to be leaving the casino and Fremont Street and too late for many new arrivals.

Pickett lived only a few blocks away to the east at the Ogden Condos, but since parking here was easier than the walk along the Fremont Street Experience this time of the night, she figured there was no point in parking at home.

For the last six months, after the Cold Poker Gang poker games at Lott and Julia's home, Pickett and her partner, Robin Sprague, had come here for a late dinner. It had become a tradition for them and they both liked the time to unwind and talk about the cold case they were working on.

During the week between games they often spent every day tracking down leads. Robin was an expert with computers, so she took that end while Pickett took the lead on the real-world stuff.

Besides, the footwork took more time and since Pickett was single and Robin married, Pickett didn't mind picking up some of that slack at all. Least she could do for her best friend who had actually managed to hold a marriage and a police career together at the same time.

That was a feat not duplicated by many.

Last week they had cleared a tough old missing person's case from the 1970s and both felt great about that. Even that old of a case gave families some closure.

And the Cold Poker Gang last week had given them a round of applause, a tradition she liked when someone closed a case. Having other detectives she admired and respected applaud her work never got old.

At this point, there were fourteen retired detectives in the Cold Poker Gang, but only about ten showed up on any given Tuesday. She and Robin had decided they wouldn't miss a night, they loved it that much.

And they loved working the cold cases. Before they retired, they never seemed to have enough time for many cold cases. That's why the Las Vegas Police Chief had given the Cold Poker Gang special status to work on cold cases. They could all still carry their guns and their badges. They just didn't get paid.

Having an unpaid group of experienced detectives volunteering to work cold cases freed up the on-duty detectives to do the more pressing work and allowed Las Vegas to now have one of the top-rated levels of closing cold cases in the entire country.

Besides that, no member of the gang had to do any paperwork. Pickett considered that the best of both worlds. She could work at her own pace, do the job she still loved, and not have to do paperwork.

She had retired and gone to police heaven, as far as she was concerned.

This week, Retired Detective Andor Williams, the Cold Poker Gang's official contact with the Chief of Police, had given her and Robin a cold murder from 2010 as their next focus case.

And Andor had suggested that Retired Detective Ben "Sarge" Carson join them on the case.

That had surprised her. Neither Pickett or Robin had met Sarge before tonight, but Pickett remembered seeing him around the main police headquarters at times over the years. And she had heard how good he was, often working alone to solve cases.

Sarge had been stationed out of the university area headquarters, out the Strip toward the airport, and she and Robin had worked out of the Sunnerlin Station to the west of downtown.

It seemed that Sarge had been an early member of the Cold Poker Gang and had been pulled away by some family crisis for a couple years, but as of tonight he was back.

Pickett had been surprised at how handsome Sarge was. He had thick, gray hair, a square jaw that looked like it had never been punched, and was solid and very much in-shape. He looked to be about her age, but she couldn't tell for sure.

Plus he had a smile that seemed natural and hit his hazel eyes every time.

And he had smiled at her when he shook her hand. For a moment she hadn't wanted to let his hand go. She hadn't felt that way about a man since long before her cheating bastard of a husband moved with his thirty-year-old secretary to Los Angeles ten years ago in a mid-life crisis that could be described as only a laughing cliché.

The bastard had paid the price. She had gotten her

wonderful three-bedroom penthouse condo in The Ogden and more than enough money to not have to work again.

So the sudden attraction to Sarge sort of flustered Pickett. He had been playing on another table. When the games broke at ten as they always did, Pickett noticed he had more chips than he started with. So he was a poker player to watch out for. She liked that.

So now he was going to join her and Robin here at the Golden Nugget for dinner to talk about their new case.

It seemed that for one case, for the first time in years, she and Robin would have a third member on their team.

And Pickett decided she didn't mind at all, if he just kept smiling and looking handsome.

# CHAPTER TWO

*October 18th, 2016*
*Las Vegas, Nevada*

Retired Detective Ben "Sarge" Carson headed across the street from the first floor of the Golden Nugget parking garage and in through the main doors by the Starbucks. He was whistling softly to himself and walking lighter than he had in years. It felt great to be back working again.

He liked the Golden Nugget more than he wanted to admit and had made it a four-times-a-week habit of coming here for the buffet at breakfast. It was an easy walk from his condo, which also helped him get out and get a little exercise as well.

The buffet had great food, reasonable prices, and friendly people. And that breakfast routine had given him some structure in his days. For the last two years, structure was what he had missed the most.

He would get up in the morning and wonder what to do with his day.

He had spent some time traveling, a long cruise, and two trips a year to New York City to see his daughter, Steph, who worked there for a magazine.

But since Andrea had divorced him five years ago and moved to Chicago with a guy she had met from work, finding some sort of structure had been an everyday project.

Sarge had retired from the force just after Andrea left and for a short time worked casino security at the MGM Grand. Also, during that year he had been a member of the Cold Poker Gang.

But even on that he couldn't keep his mind focused. There was just something about a woman he trusted and loved and lived with for over thirty years suddenly just saying she was leaving and moving in with another man.

In hindsight, he could see all the signs. He had worked more and more, stayed away from home more and more, because it just wasn't pleasant to be home once Steph had gone off to college.

And Andrea had worked more and more and they barely saw each other the last few years. He knew, in his heart, the marriage was over. He just hadn't wanted to admit it.

He admired Andrea for taking the step to clear things out. He wasn't angry at her and actually liked the guy she moved with to Chicago. She wasn't the problem.

He was the problem. He just couldn't figure out what to do with his life at sixty-two years of age. So he had sold their family home, given half of the proceeds to Andrea, then bought a penthouse condo in the Ogden using just a tiny, tiny bit of his inheritance money from his father who had died the year before. Sarge loved the condo, but still needed a great deal more in his life.

Tonight, being back with the detectives of the Cold Poker

Gang and talking solving crimes had felt wonderful. He knew he had found at least a part of what he had been looking for.

As Lott had said to him when they talked about Sarge rejoining the Cold Poker Gang, "It gives life a purpose."

Sarge could feel that clearly tonight.

And then Andor had suggested he join up with Pickett and Sprague, the two best women detectives ever to work the Las Vegas streets. Sarge had been surprised at that, but when Sarge heard what the case was, he had almost hugged Andor.

Andor had known Sarge was coming back, so he had pulled a cold case that Andor knew Sarge had a personal connection with.

The "Wedding Dress Murder" as it had been called, had been Sarge's case originally. And not solving that poor girl's murder had bothered him more than he wanted to admit over the years.

Now, with two of the best detectives the city had to offer, just recently retired, he was finally going to have the time to run at the "Wedding Dress Murder" as it should have been.

And that just had him whistling and smiling.

It was time to get back to work, time to do what he had loved once again.

# CHAPTER THREE

*October 18th, 2016*
*Las Vegas, Nevada*

When Pickett got to the restaurant, Robin was already sitting at their favorite booth in the back of the twenty-four hour café on the main floor of the hotel. The restaurant, in the last remodel, had gone from being open with hundreds of tables to being smaller, but much nicer.

Now the booth was cloth-covered brown tones with nice wood tabletop and plants between the booths giving a feeling of privacy. The restaurant staff were always friendly, and at ten in the evening they had switched over to their late-night menu which was mostly sandwiches, desserts, a few steaks, and break-fasts of all kinds. All of it good.

Usually Robin sat on one side of the booth with her back to a kitchen door and Pickett sat on the other, but tonight Robin had scooted around to the back of the booth to give Sarge one side when he arrived.

Retired Detective Robin Sprague was about as tough a cop as there was, and Pickett had zero doubt Robin was a lot smarter than she was.

Robin was square and solid, with arms and shoulders of a swimmer even at sixty. She often spent time swimming as exercise and had competed in some senior's events. She kept her gray hair cut short and often wore a wide-billed baseball cap to keep the sun off her face.

Pickett burned easily in the sun, while Robin seldom seemed to use suntan lotion and just seemed to tan evenly as the summer went on. They had been partners for over twenty years since both were promoted to detective at the same time.

Robin had one kid, now back east working in Washington. And her husband, Will, still ran one of Las Vegas's top security firms. He managed to keep safe some of the most powerful and famous people on the planet every day.

Besides that, he was one of the nicest men Pickett had ever had the pleasure to meet. After Pickett's divorce, Robin and Will had almost adopted her, asking her over for all kinds of things to keep her mind occupied.

Wonderful friends that didn't come any better.

"So what do you think of working with Sarge?" Robin asked as Pickett slid into her normal side of the booth and took a sip from the glass of ice water already there.

"I think it's going to be fun, actually," Pickett said. And she did think that.

"Because he's a hunk?" Robin asked, smiling.

Pickett knew that smile and that evil grin from her partner.

Pickett laughed. "There's that. But if I remember right, he's married."

"Nope," Robin said, still holding that evil grin. "Divorced right before he retired five years ago."

Now that sat Pickett back in her seat. She had been instantly attracted to Sarge tonight. And he was available.

"Seriously?" Pickett asked.

"You can ask him yourself," Robin said, indicating the entrance to the restaurant.

Sarge had just come in and spotted them in the back. Pickett watched him weave through the tables, his solid form moving with an ease that you didn't often see in someone at his age. He seemed completely in control of himself and his movements.

Pickett could feel her stomach clamp up at watching him. Damn, he had to be the most handsome man in downtown Las Vegas. How the hell was it possible she was even attracted to him? She had figured that part of her life was done. It certainly had been shut off for a lot of years.

And Sarge was smiling as he reached the table and nodded. "Detectives."

Robin indicated that he should join them and he did. The wonderful smile never left his face.

"You win tonight?" Robin asked as Sarge sat down.

All Pickett could do was just stare at him, so she was glad her partner picked up the slack for the moment.

"Being able to work with you two is a win in my book," Sarge said.

"Now that's smooth," Pickett said, smiling.

"Oh, I like him already," Robin said, laughing.

"Yup, me too," Pickett said.

And then Sarge looked up into her eyes and she damn near forgot to breathe. His hazel eyes just held her and she decided right at that moment all she really wanted to do was just stare into his eyes.

He seemed frozen for a moment as well, then laughed and said, "And I won forty bucks as well."

And that broke the ice and the intense moment and Pickett actually managed to take a drink of water without her hands shaking. She was very proud of that fact.

# CHAPTER FOUR

*October 18th, 2016*
*Las Vegas, Nevada*

Sarge was stunned at how attracted he felt instantly to Pickett. Her brown eyes had held his gaze and she seemed to see everything about him. He hadn't had a reaction like that in memory toward a woman. Nothing that was that kind of instant and strong.

Now he hoped he didn't make a fool of himself working with them. She was considered the best woman detective who ever wore a badge in Las Vegas. Maybe one of the best detectives ever, period. And her partner Robin was almost as good. He was way outclassed with this partnership.

They gave their drink orders to a kind woman with tinted blue hair and tattoos on both arms and then Sarge decided he needed to get things clear as quickly as possible.

"I bet you are wondering why Andor suggested I work with you two on this new case."

"It did seem surprising," Pickett said, nodding.

Damn, her voice was thick and rich and had a wonderful throaty sound to it. He loved that.

"Andor did it as a favor to me because I was coming back to the gang," Sarge said. "The Wedding Dress Murder was my case originally. Driven me nuts for years. Haunted me, actually."

Robin laughed and sat back, shaking her head. Pickett just kept smiling, a smile that reached her eyes and Sarge wouldn't mind seeing a lot more of that.

"Wow, do we know that feeling," Robin said.

Pickett nodded. "I still have nightmares about a couple of our cold cases. But Andor doesn't want us to tackle them yet."

"I trust Andor and Lott and Julia," Sarge said. "That's why when he gave you two the new case tonight, he suggested I might be able to help. I think he figured I wouldn't get anywhere with it alone and you two could crack it."

"You didn't know he was going to give that case to us?" Robin asked.

"Not a clue," Sarge said. "Surprised and pleased me. I thought about giving Andor a hug, but figured I would never live that down."

Both detectives broke into laughter and Sarge could feel the tension easing.

"Damn," Robin said, "I would give anything to see you hug Andor."

"We solve this case and you might get your wish," Sarge said.

"Oh, that is so a deal," Pickett said, laughing.

At that moment the waitress came back with their drinks and they all ordered. Sarge went with a straight cheeseburger while Pickett had a Denver Omelet and Robin had a club sandwich that she said she would take home half to her husband.

Sarge decided he needed to figure out how he was going to fit in with a long-term working team.

"So, how do the two of you work together?" Sarge asked. "And how can I help and stay out of the way at the same time?"

Pickett smiled at him with that question. Clearly she appreciated it.

"I'm the computer geek and I have a husband," Robin said. "So I often let Pickett do the field work and I do the tracking online."

"And I like the field work," Pickett said. "More than I want to admit at times."

"I do too," Sarge said. "Banging on doors and face-to-face questions can sometimes work wonders."

"So looks like you join Pickett," Robin said. "You got a problem with that, partner?"

Sarge watched as Pickett smiled back at her partner, then turned to Sarge with the same smile that reached her wonderful brown eyes. "No problem at all."

"Perfect," Robin said.

Sarge nodded. "Perfect by me as well. Just don't let me slow you down."

Pickett nodded. "Oh trust me, I won't."

He had a hunch that was the truest statement he had heard in a long, long time. He was really, really starting to like this woman and he didn't even know her.

# CHAPTER FIVE

*October 18th, 2016*
Las Vegas, Nevada

"Notebook," Pickett said to Robin, signaling that they were going to get to work.

Robin brought up onto the table from beside her a blue spiral-bound notebook and the file folder for the case.

Pickett was excited about this new case and actually excited to get to work with Sarge. And to get to know him better. Two cops out pounding the pavement together definitely got to know each other fairly quickly.

And he had sure said all the right things so far, telling them up front why he was with them and also asking about their methods to see how he would fit in. Both of those had impressed her.

"We use a notebook when we are talking to try to think out our plans and leads," Robin said.

"Amazing how that helps us be organized," Pickett said.

Sarge smiled and pulled a small notebook out of his back pocket and flipped it open. "Can't agree more. If I don't write a thought down these days, it pretends to never have existed and goes and hides."

Pickett laughed. "Damn, do I know that feeling."

"So what can you tell us about this case?" Robin asked.

"Damn near nothing that's not in the file there," Sarge said, shaking his head. "And it's a thin file I'm afraid."

Pickett could see that really, really bothered him. He actually cared about cases like she did. Another thing she liked about him already.

"The victim's name was Trudy Patterson," Sarge said without looking at the file that Robin had opened. "She was twenty-five and from Denver."

He took a sip of water and then went on.

"She was in Vegas by herself for three days planning a wedding and on May 17th, 2010, she left her suite in the MGM Grand to run a few errands and was never seen alive again."

"Did you find her?" Pickett asked.

Sarge nodded. "Five days later her body was found in her rental car sitting on a bluff overlooking Vegas to the west. She was wearing a wedding dress, but not the one she planned on wearing for her wedding."

"I don't see a cause of death," Robin said, glancing at the file.

"Impossible to determine," Sarge said. "We ruled out all the normal causes such as blunt force trauma and obvious wounds. She had been sitting in the closed-up car, in the heat, dead for days. It wasn't a pretty sight. But there didn't seem to be any obvious injuries to her or any sign of sexual activity, from what could be figured out from the decomposing body. In fact, it's not even officially a murder."

DEAN WESLEY SMITH

Pickett knew for certain now this was a case that had haunted Sarge. He hadn't even glanced at the file and yet remembered all the details after six years. She had a couple cases that ate at her like that as well.

"Family all clear?" Robin asked, still glancing at the file.

"Completely," Sarge said. "They were the ones that insisted to me, sometimes at the top of their voices, that this wasn't just a woman who got cold feet and ran away from a wedding. That something horrid had happened to her."

"But you checked all of them anyway?" Pickett asked, smiling at Sarge.

He smiled back. "I would have found a flea on one of them if it was there. Nothing. They all loved her and she seemed to have no other enemies at all."

"Wedding dress?" Pickett asked, staring at Sarge. He must have gone down that road as well.

"She was about to be married and we found her in a wedding dress," Sarge said. "So I chased that down as much as I could. The dress she was found in was a standard one that could be bought in a hundred stores and nothing in her planning seemed to connect in any way to anyone of interest. And nothing in her financial records showed that she bought the dress she was wearing when we found her."

"But that's where we start digging," Robin said, writing in her notebook.

"Agreed," Sarge said. "I kept feeling I was missing something in her wedding planning, but could never put my finger on it."

Pickett watched as Sarge seemed to vanish into his own thoughts for a moment, his handsome face very serious.

"So why did this case become the one that haunted you?" Pickett asked.

"I have a daughter named Steph who lives in New York,"

24

Sarge said. "Steph was talking about getting married and was only two years younger than Trudy Patterson at the time of the murder."

Pickett sat back, nodding.

"So how did the wedding go?" Robin asked.

"Thankfully, they eloped to Hawaii," Sarge said.

Pickett laughed and then leaned forward. "With a little financial help from Dad I bet?"

He just lit up smiling and shaking his head. "I must plead the fifth on that."

Pickett laughed and at that moment the food came and let Sarge off the hook.

# CHAPTER SIX

*October 18th, 2016*
*Las Vegas, Nevada*

As they ate and talked about different things, Sarge found himself relaxing more and more with Pickett and Robin. Both were smart, funny, and focused.

It was about halfway through the meal that the conversation turned back to the case at hand. He decided he needed to give them the questions that had puzzled him from the start.

"So my biggest question about this case has always been why the dress?" Sarge said. "Did the killer, if she was actually killed, know she was going to be married and did the killer find her through something she did in the marriage preparation?"

Robin nodded and wrote all that down.

"No traction on those questions I assume?" Pickett asked.

"Nothing," Pickett said. "And right up until I retired I was still trying to retrace some of Trudy's movements in the three days ahead of her disappearance and murder. Nothing. I have my notebook full of all that at home. I would have brought it, but didn't realize I would be working on this case tonight."

Pickett smiled. "Glad we are."

"So am I," Sarge said, smiling back at her.

For a moment they stared at each other. Sarge felt as if Pickett was looking into his every secret. And he honestly didn't mind.

"Why did it take her so long to be found?" Robin asked, breaking the moment between him and Pickett. "Makes no sense if she was sitting up there in the car for days. I'm familiar with that bluff area and it gets a lot of traffic because of the view."

"She was strapped in and upright in the car in the driver's seat," Sarge said, remembering clearly the image of Trudy's body in that hot, hot car. "So we think no one thought anything was wrong. It wasn't until a couple on foot walked past the car that they noticed she was dead and called it in and we connected the car to the missing person's case."

"Similar cases?" Pickett asked.

"I had a couple people try to dig up what they could," Sarge said, "but I honestly don't think we covered that very well."

"That's going to change," Robin said, writing in the notebook.

Sarge looked at her and then at Pickett, who was smiling.

"Robin's husband is Will Sprague," Pickett said.

"Oh," Sarge said. He knew of Will Sprague, the head of Sprague Securities, the best security agency in the city. He ran an entire force of retired Special Forces men and women to protect the rich and famous. He did everything aboveboard and worked closely with the police at times for major events.

Plus Sarge knew that Sprague had more money than almost anyone in this city, and that was going some.

Plus Sarge knew that Sprague had more money than almost anyone in this city, and that was going some.

"We have an entire office suite full of the best computer people on the planet," Robin said. "If this case hooks up at all to any other, we'll find the connection."

Sarge laughed. "I sure got with the right team here."

"We like solving cases," Pickett said.

"Damn right we do," Robin said. "So a couple more questions I'm not seeing here in the report. Was Trudy fully dressed under the wedding dress?"

"No," Sarge said. "And no sign of the clothes she was wearing when she left the hotel either."

"It says here she had on a wedding ring," Robin said.

"She did?" Pickett asked, leaning forward.

"She did," Sarge said, nodding. "And her family insisted they had never seen the ring before. All it had was a number two-seventy-three etched inside."

The two women looked at each other and Sarge watched the clear communication of years of being partners.

"What are you thinking?" he asked.

"The killer married Trudy," Pickett said. "Before killing her."

Robin nodded.

Sarge sat back. He had always wondered if it was something like that, but having Pickett and Robin both jump instantly to that conclusion confirmed his suspicions.

He turned to Robin. "That's the link to other cases you want to search for."

"Damn, you're right," Robin said, writing in her notebook.

Sarge glanced at Pickett who was smiling at him.

And he liked that smile more than he wanted to admit, even to himself.

# THE TRAIL EXPLODES

# CHAPTER SEVEN

*October 19th, 2016*
*Las Vegas, Nevada*

Pickett was surprised at how comfortable the Golden Nugget Buffet was, and how wonderful it smelled at ten in the morning. Eggs, bacon, with a background smell of waffles and maple syrup. She got instantly hungry just getting near the place.

Sarge said he ate here four mornings a week and just approaching the place gave her an idea why. The buffet was up an escalator away from the casino and then surrounded by planters with tall green plants under the high ceiling.

The far wall was all windows that looked out over the large main-floor pool and shark tank below. Those windows really made the entire place feel almost like sitting on a balcony instead of in a dark casino.

Everything was oak and brown-toned cloth and there were more than enough tables to hold a fairly large crowd. At this point, there weren't more than thirty people scattered around the restaurant and Sarge sat at a table off to one side, reading the morning newspaper.

He had a cup of coffee in front of him, but no food.

She read the same paper, but always on her iPad in the mornings. She smiled at how handsome he looked sitting there, clearly absorbed in the reading.

As she neared the front desk, he glanced up and waved to her over the planter that she should just come in. She did, going past the cash register and a smiling woman hostess who just nodded to her.

He stood as she approached, the smile reaching his eyes.

Again, she was struck at how really, really handsome he was and how attracted to him she had become in just one day. And he had manners. She couldn't remember the last time a person had stood for her when she approached a table.

"You didn't need to buy me breakfast," she said, smiling at him as she sat down and he sat back down as well. "But thank you."

He laughed. "I didn't. But maybe I should take the credit."

"Do I need to go pay?" She glanced back at the cashiers who didn't seem to even notice she was sitting down.

"Nope," he said, holding up what looked like a ticket to a show on the Strip. "I eat here so often, they keep giving me two-for-one coupons, but until today I never had a chance to use one."

"Glad I could be of service," she said, laughing.

"Then let's eat," he said, standing.

Ten minutes later they were back at the table. Both had personally-made ham-and-cheese omelets and she had some fruit and a small slice of a waffle. He had gone for a slice of ham and two strips of bacon with his omelet.

"I can see why you like this place," she said. "Lots of choices of food, comfortable place with lots of light, and friendly people."

"I have a hunch I would eat here seven mornings a week if I let myself," he said, shaking his head.

"And what would be wrong with that?" she asked, biting in to the fantastic omelet and savoring the taste.

"Just never imagined myself in my early sixties being in a rut like this," he said.

"Honestly," she said, smiling at the slight look of worry in his eyes. "I like morning routines. With all the craziness of being a cop during the day, my only sane time was mornings."

"Yeah," he said, nodding. "That I agree with. Just feels wrong doing it alone I guess."

Pickett understood that as well. She wanted to get to know this man better and she was known for being blunt, so no time to fade on that now.

"So divorced, huh?" Picket asked. "Do you have more than one daughter?"

"Just the one," Sarge said, the grin returning to his face as he said that. "She's amazing."

"Tough divorce?" Pickett asked.

Sarge shook his head as he kept eating. "Actually, no. Andrea and I had drifted apart as this job tends to do to people. She met a nice guy and decided she wanted to start over just as I retired. I like the guy she met and she and I are still friends. They live in Chicago."

Pickett actually sat back with that. Sarge just kept eating and she could tell there was no emotional energy at all talking about his ex-wife. He really did still get along with her.

Pickett was really, really liking this man more and more.

"So how about you?" Sarge said, glancing up and noticing that she had stopped eating and was staring at him.

"Wonderful daughter living in Washington, DC," Pickett said. "My husband had a midlife crisis and went off to LA with a twenty-some-year-old and a new red sports car. I got enough money to live comfortably the rest of my life and a wonderful condo in the Ogden, all paid off."

"Wow," Sarge said, staring at her. He seemed surprised about something for a moment. Then he said, "Seems you are over it because I heard no anger there at all."

Pickett shrugged. "Only time I got angry was at him being so stupid. I don't do well with stupidity in general, but especially from him. So I made him pay to get rid of me and it hasn't bothered me much since."

Sarge laughed and kept staring at her, smiling.

"I got egg on my nose or something?" Pickett asked, after a moment, pretending to wipe off her face. She loved it when he looked at her like that.

"Nope," he said. "just admiring someone who I have a lot in common with. Me and stupidity are not friends either."

"Oh, God," Pickett said, going back to eating. "Heaven help a poor fool who runs into us together."

"Doubt heaven would help him," Sarge said, laughing.

Pickett laughed as well. Damn, how was this man even possible?

But it seemed he was.

# CHAPTER EIGHT

*October 19th, 2016*
*Las Vegas, Nevada*

Sarge couldn't remember the last time he had enjoyed a breakfast as much as this one with Pickett. Not only was she the best-looking woman he had met, but she was funny, and smart, and a fantastic detective.

And she liked the Golden Nugget Buffet.

He wasn't honestly sure which of those things scared him more about her. But he was going to just enjoy the time with her as he had it and see what happened.

After breakfast, she had pulled out a notebook and he had taken his small notebook out of his back pocket with his notes about the case, and they set to work.

"I haven't heard from Robin yet about any of the searches she is doing," Pickett said. "So got any ideas as to where we start?"

Sarge liked the sounds of the "we" part of that. He had

been fighting this case so long on his own, it felt fantastic to have top help with it.

"I had an idea about six months ago I haven't been able to do anything about yet," Sarge said. "How about we detail out what a woman like Trudy would need to do to prepare for a wedding here in Las Vegas, then eliminate the stops she already made to figure out what her errands might have been the day she disappeared?"

Pickett brightened up with that. "I like that a lot. Somewhere on one of those last errands is where things went bad for her."

"Exactly," Sarge said. "But who do we know that would be able to detail out a Las Vegas wedding like that? My daughter eloped."

Pickett smiled. "Robin and I have a friend who could do that easily. So let's put together the details we know that Trudy did before she disappeared, then head there."

"Your friend wouldn't happen to be Elvis?" Sarge asked, poking at her.

"Nope," Pickett said, smiling at Sarge. "Elvis's wife. Didn't you know, Elvis is dead?"

Sarge just laughed and shook his head. Then they spent the next thirty minutes putting together every detail that was known about Trudy's three days in Las Vegas and what parts of her wedding details she had already taken care of.

Then, with to-go cups full of fresh coffee offered by a friendly waitress, they headed out to Pickett's car, a blue Grand Cherokee SUV parked on the second level of the parking garage.

Sarge buckled into the passenger seat and tried to remember the last time he had ridden with someone to go anywhere. With him and Andrea, he had always driven.

And with the rotating partners he had over the years, he had always been the main driver. It felt very, very weird to be in the passenger seat, that was for sure.

But Pickett got them out of the garage easily and merging into traffic without a problem. She drove one-handed, with a confidence of a long-time driver who just knew where to look and when. After a few blocks, he relaxed completely. More than likely she was a better driver than he was.

Was there anything at all wrong with this woman?

The chapel they were headed to was on the Stratosphere end of the Strip, closest to downtown, so the drive only took about five minutes. Pickett pulled the SUV into a small parking lot behind a building with a giant Elvis holding a wedding ring on the front. Damn, she hadn't been kidding. They really were going to an Elvis chapel.

The business looked like it had seen better days and needed a coat of paint, at least. A gutter was hanging loose off of one side and some graffiti scarred up another wall. Sarge just couldn't imagine anyone wanting to get married in such a shabby place. But it was Las Vegas, so anything was possible.

The sun was starting to get warm already and Pickett pulled out a baseball cap from the back seat and made sure the wide bill shaded her face.

"I burn instantly," she said, shaking her head.

Sarge laughed. "You ought to see the hat I wear in the summer. The brim is so wide all the way around, my daughter told me I look like a villain from a spaghetti western."

Pickett laughed as they opened the large front door of the building. The door had a stained-glass window in the middle that hadn't been cleaned in months, at least.

The inside was cool and dark and smelled slightly moldy. A background smell of old cigarettes covered everything. To Sarge the place felt more like a run-down mortuary than a wedding chapel. There were some overstuffed couches around a waiting room with dark-wood paneling and cheap end tables covered in ashtrays. Two of the ashtrays were still full of cigarette butts.

Sarge had no desire at all to sit on the couches. God-only-knew what was on them, considering he could see patterns of stains in places waiting-room couches should not be stained.

There were no signs, no pricing, no images of Elvis anywhere in the room. Just a plain room with dark wood paneling and ugly maroon couches. This really had to be the worst wedding chapel he had ever been in.

A heavy-set woman came out of the back door. She had on a pink print dress that looked faded and a beehive hairdo that seemed to defy gravity.

Her hair was a bright silver and her face had what looked like built-up layers of make-up. Her eyes had so much dark make-up around them, she looked like a distant relative of a raccoon.

"Detective Pickett," the woman said, her voice hoarse like a person who smoked far, far too many cigarettes. "What a welcome surprise on a dull morning."

"Business bad?" Pickett asked.

The woman shrugged and the hair towering on her head didn't even shake. "Got five weddings this week I'm working on around town, but that's slow."

Pickett turned to Sarge. "This is Detective Carson," Pickett said. "Detective, this is Madeline Stein, just Stein to all her friends. She's the best wedding planner in the city."

"Nice meeting you," Sarge said, nodding to the woman who nodded back at him and seemed pleased at Pickett's description of her, but not surprised.

"So we have an old cold case we're working on," Pickett

said. "We had a woman back in the spring of 2010 go missing right near the end of planning her wedding."

The woman nodded, the tower of silver hair staying firm on her head, and Pickett went on. Sarge was going to let her lead on this one all the way.

"We have traced most of everything the woman did before she disappeared. But we are wondering what she would have left to do."

Stein smiled. "To see who the woman planning her wedding was going to visit when she vanished to give you some leads, huh?"

"Exactly," Pickett said.

"You got a list of what she already had done?"

Sarge handed Stein the list. "This is what we know she did and in the order she did it."

Stein scanned down the list quickly, nodding. Then she looked up and asked, "Do you know if her dress needed a fitting?"

"Already done before she came into town," Sarge said.

Stein nodded again and once again the tower of hair didn't seem to even shake, let alone threaten to fall off her head. The thing had to be wired up there somehow. No hair could hold that shape without a lot of help.

"The woman was a good planner," Stein said. "She did everything exactly right and in the right order. Right out of my book, actually."

Sarge was surprised at that mention of a book, but said nothing.

"So if she was following your book," Pickett asked. "What last-minute things did she need to do?"

"Could be a number of things," Stein said.

Sarge took out his notebook as Stein started to list things Trudy Patterson might have done that final day.

"If she was alone in town, she might have been taking care of the groom's tux."

"She was alone," Pickett said.

"She would have checked on the flowers she ordered," Stein said. "She would have had a final appointment with the wedding chapel and she might have wanted to set up limos for the guests arriving at the airport."

Stein handed the list back to Sarge and turned to Pickett. "Was this woman ever found?"

"Five days later," Pickett said, "In her car."

"Wearing a wedding dress with nothing under it and a ring no one had seen before with a number on the ring," Stein said.

Sarge damn near staggered backwards. How in the world did this woman know that?

Pickett seemed rocked as well. "Stein, how did you know all that?"

"Did the girl give a description of her rapist?" Stein asked.

"She was dead," Pickett said.

"Sat for days in a hot car," Sarge said.

"Oh, the poor girl," Stein said, shaking her head. "Never heard of any of them dying before."

"Them?" Pickett and Sarge said both at the same time.

"Sure," Stein said. "I can give you a list of the ones I remember. But I'm sure they all filed rape reports, or at least most of them. The bastard doing that cost all of us planners and chapels around town a lot of business over the years and you folks could never get a lead on him. When the bride gets raped right before a wedding, the wedding always gets called off."

Pickett and Sarge just looked at each other. Sarge felt like he was in shock.

Stein laughed a throaty, deep laugh. "You two are surprised, I can tell."

"We are," Pickett said. "We are homicide detectives, so we didn't follow much else."

"And this case never linked to any rape cases," Sarge said.

"I think the detectives who came by here a few times called the guy the Bride Rapist."

"Any cases lately?" Pickett asked.

"I've heard of one or two," Stein said, nodding. "Might want to check with some of the bigger chapels and with your own folks."

Sarge just couldn't believe what he was hearing. His one case, his nightmare case, had just gotten a lot, lot bigger.

And even more nightmarish.

# CHAPTER NINE

*October 19th, 2016*
*Las Vegas, Nevada*

Pickett didn't say anything after they thanked Stein for her time and headed toward her car. The heat of the morning was picking up and the parking lot pavement made it worse.

As she unlocked her car and climbed in, she called Robin, then turned on the car to get it cooled down.

Sarge climbed into the passenger seat and closed the door as Robin came on the line and Pickett switched the phone to speaker so they could both listen.

"Sarge and I discovered something huge," Pickett said before Robin could say anything but "Hi, partner."

It took Pickett about three minutes to explain what they had just discovered from Stein, including the stops Trudy might have taken the morning she vanished.

When Pickett finished, Robin was silent for a long moment.

The only sounds were the air-conditioning and the traffic on the nearby Strip.

Finally Robin said, "Jesus, the poor girl."

"I'm betting we're not dealing with a purposeful murder," Pickett said.

Beside her, Sarge was nodding.

"She was raped right before her wedding," Robin said, "so in shock she went up to that ridge and just sat and passed out and died from the heat."

"Exactly," Pickett said.

"That just makes me sick," Robin said. "But we still take this bastard down for her death."

"Agreed," Sarge said.

Pickett couldn't agree more. Her stomach was twisted up like she was staring at a freshly-opened grave. She hated that more than anything, and this felt exactly like that.

Again the silence was broken only by the air-conditioning hum and the street noise. It seemed like a very heavy silence.

Sarge just stared at his notebook.

"So you want us to go get the files from the sexual crimes unit on all of the cases?" Pickett asked.

"I can do that easily from here," Robin said. "I'm going to get one or two of our computer people on this, searching for patterns, anything that might give this sicko away."

"We'll follow up on the leads that Stein gave us that Trudy might have done that last morning," Pickett said. "Let us know at once if a pattern starts to emerge so we can focus down."

"Got it," Robin said.

And she hung up.

Pickett clicked off the phone and turned to face the handsome detective beside her. His expression was one of determination.

"Suggestions on which thing Trudy did that we tackle first?" Pickett asked.

Sarge nodded and looked at her, his hazel eyes intent. "Since there are so many, and all of the cases are around weddings of some sort, I'm thinking that narrows it down to the flowers or the tuxes or the chapel."

Pickett nodded. "Tuxes. That kind of shop would also have access to wedding dresses."

"Good place to start," Sarge said, nodding.

He flipped open his notebook and went through it quickly until he reached a page about halfway through. "August's Tux Place."

Picket was impressed that he had taken that detailed of notes.

"I went in there," Sarge said, "but they claimed to have never seen her that day."

"Of course they did," Pickett said.

Then she realized there was a huge bit of data they didn't have. They were so used to working homicides where the victims couldn't talk, it just dawned on her that there were survivors. From what Stein had said, a lot of them.

"We need the information from the survivors first," Pickett said. "See what they remember."

"Of course," Sarge said, shaking his head.

Pickett smiled. A homicide detective seldom had survivors to talk with.

Pickett called Robin back and asked her to quickly scan a bunch of the reports to see how the rape victims were taken. That alone would narrow their focus.

"Give me three minutes," Robin said and again hung up.

Pickett glanced over at Sarge, who was staring at his notebook.

"Anything there that make sense with this new information?"

Sarge nodded. "No real clear cause of death. Now that makes sense. And why she was on that ridge makes sense now as well. So many questions suddenly answered as a ton more questions pop up."

Pickett looked at the handsome detective. Then she said, "Why do I have the suspicion this is bigger than even a serial rapist?"

"I was thinking the same thing," Sarge said, glancing at her. "Not a clue why, however. But my gut is twisted on this one, which tells me we're missing a lot of this."

Pickett knew that feeling as well. And as detectives, you learned to trust that gut. Sometimes your subconscious could see things your waking mind couldn't see. Someone had once explained to her that was what "gut sense" meant. She just knew she had learned to trust hers.

At that moment Robin called back and Pickett clicked on the phone.

"No help," Robin said.

"How can there be no help?" Pickett asked. "That makes no sense at all."

"That's what has stumped the detectives working these cases," Robin said. "The women have no memory at all on the day they were taken."

"Any record of some of them being hypnotized to bring up lost memories?" Sarge asked.

"Six of them that I can tell tried that," Robin said. "I'm still digging, but what the pattern is that the women seem to remember is leaving for an errand on their own, then waking up as they are being married to a tall man wearing a plastic face in some sort of wedding chapel. They are drugged and can't speak or even talk. Then they are taken to a nearby bedroom and raped, then the next thing they remember, they are in their cars."

"Drugs," Sarge said a moment before Pickett could.

"That's the theory on this," Robin said, "but no drugs were found in the women's systems in any fashion. No DNA traces, nothing."

"So we have someone who knows chemicals and drugs," Pickett said.

"You said they were married?" Sarge asked Robin. "Someone else there?"

"Yes," Robin said. "A third person was always involved in the ceremony wearing an Elvis mask and dressed like Elvis."

Sarge glanced over at the Elvis chapel at the same time Pickett did.

Then Pickett decided she needed to quickly ask Robin one more question to make sure Stein was cleared.

"Any description of the groom or the Elvis person besides the masks?"

"Both extremely thin," Robin said after a moment. "And a lot of the victims have a memory of a smell of roses."

Pickett just shook her head. This was beyond strange and ugly.

Then Sarge twisted it one more twist.

"Robin, would it be possible for your people to review missing persons' cases where a near-future bride went missing. I know I dealt with a lot of them and always thought it was just the bride getting cold feet."

Pickett looked at Sarge who was frowning and intent. "You think the women who were set free are only the tip of this?"

"I have a hunch," Sarge said. "And Robin, if not too much problem, add in the men who vanished right before getting married as well."

"Crap, just crap," Robin said. "I'll get more people on this. Back with you two as soon as I can."

And Robin hung up.

"God, I hope you are wrong on this hunch," Pickett said.

"So do I," Sarge said.

He turned and looked at her intently. "But you don't think I am, do you?"

"No," Pickett said.

And she hated that more than she wanted to admit.

# CHAPTER TEN

*October 19th, 2016*
*Las Vegas, Nevada*

Sarge glanced at Pickett, then back at the Elvis chapel. "Is Stein some sort of marriage expert?"

"Wrote the major book on how to get married in Las Vegas," Pickett said.

"What's with this old chapel?" Sarge asked.

"It's not used anymore," Pickett said. "Stein's husband, Bernie, was the Elvis here who married people and kept the building up. He died of a heart attack about twelve years ago and Stein wrote her book and then started freelancing for other chapels and numbers of the casinos."

"How much do you trust her?"

"She helped Robin and me on more cases than I want to count," Pickett said. "So a lot. She knows weddings and a lot about the darker sides of this city. She and Bernie lived and worked here through the mob days."

Sarge nodded. They were going to have to trust someone at some point and if Pickett thought Stein good, they might as well trust her for the moment.

"I think we need more information about Elvis chapels," Sarge said, "why they came about, and if Stein has an estimate of how many marriages are performed in Las Vegas every year."

"Robin can get us the license information easily from the Clark County clerk," Pickett said. "But how many actually happen would be another number completely. Stein might have a guess on that."

Sarge nodded and then climbed out into the heat. The day still wasn't that warm and chances are would end up being one of those really wonderful fall days that Vegas had a lot of. Not too hot, not cold at night. Spring and fall here were the best times, and over the years Sarge had really come to appreciate the nice days.

Sarge held the large front door for Pickett and she nodded to him and gave him that wonderful smile he was coming to really enjoy as they entered the lobby.

Stein appeared almost at once, her white beehive hair still towering over her like a magic act. This time she smelled more of smoke, as if she had just crushed out a cigarette. Sarge stared at her hair for a moment trying to figure out, without success, what held the thing up. Maybe it really was magic.

"Saw you two still sitting out there on the security cam," Stein said. "Figured you would be back. What can I help you with?"

Pickett gave Stein a quick summary of some of the information, including the rape victims remembering being married by a tall man in an Elvis mask.

Stein just shook her head at that. Sarge could tell that upset her, but didn't surprise her.

"So how did this Elvis marrying people come about?" Sarge asked. "Always wondered, never knew."

"Elvis and Pricilla got married here in the old Alladin Hotel in 1967," Stein said. "That started it all and it became a thing to attract tourists who wanted to get married, just like drive-through weddings and underwater weddings and all of that."

Sarge nodded. Vegas was the home of the Elvis impersonators, so it made sense from that side as well.

"So how many marriages actually happen in Vegas every year?" Pickett asked.

Stein shrugged. "Not a clue, actually. Every casino, hotel, and small place like this one can perform them. To be able to perform a legal marriage all it takes is a simple license from the state that anyone can get for a small fee."

"Isn't there more?" Pickett asked, sounding surprised.

Sarge was surprised at that as well.

Stein shrugged. "Not much. Each couple needs to get a license from Clark County, and I think there are over eighty thousand or so of those a year normally. You can file for that online and just pick it up with proper ID when you get here. Very easy and cheap. But not sure how many of those marriages actually happened and were legally filed after they did."

Pickett nodded. "Robin should be able to find that number if we need it.

"I heard one place claim," Stein said, "that on average there were over three hundred weddings every day here. But the math on that doesn't work out compared to the licenses. I would estimate about two hundred a day is closer to the number."

Sarge just shook his head. Two-hundred weddings a day. No wonder the industry around weddings was so huge in this city.

"So how regular do either the bride or the groom get cold feet and vanish?" Pickett asked.

Sarge was impressed she had managed to stay on topic. He was still lost in the number of weddings.

"All the time," Stein said, shaking her head. "All the time."

"So much so that it's normal?" Sarge asked.

"Completely normal," Stein said. "Maybe one out of four weddings don't make it to the final kiss."

"Oh, god," Pickett said.

Sarge felt his gut clinch.

"Why?" Stein asked, looking worried and puzzled.

"We think our rapist might be doing more than raping women," Pickett said. "Just our gut sense."

Stein's face got even whiter, if that was possible under her layers of makeup, and she bent forward.

And once again, her hair remained solid and in place.

# CHAPTER ELEVEN

*October 19th, 2016*
*Las Vegas, Nevada*

Pickett led Sarge out to her Jeep and they both climbed in and she got the air-conditioning going again. She just felt stunned at how large this had become. It was no wonder the detectives investigating the rapes hadn't gotten anywhere.

"So now where?" Sarge asked. "I honestly have no idea where to even jab a stick into a mess this big."

Pickett laughed and nodded. "I have no idea either."

"So until we hear from Robin and all her computer geeks," Sarge said, "let's try August's Tux Shop. Nothing to lose at this point."

"Don't let Robin hear you call her computer people geeks," Pickett said, laughing as she backed the car around to head back out onto the Strip.

"What does she call them?" Sarge asked.

"Elves," Pickett said, grinning at Sarge before pulling into traffic. "But she's the only one allowed to and only with me."

"Got it," Sarge said, laughing.

Pickett drove, really enjoying how having Sarge beside her made her relax. She usually got all wound up in a case about this point and stressed, but his humor and just solid presence beside her made her stay level and focused. And that felt damn good.

She was really, really starting to be attracted to this man and she hadn't even known him for a full day yet. She wasn't sure how that was possible, but she sure wasn't going to slow it down. She could see no point in that in the slightest.

And even better, he seemed attracted to her. And at times they almost seemed to think the same.

It took her about ten minutes to get them into the parking lot of August's Tux Shop just off the Strip. It was a clean, modern, single-story building with windows across the front full of different forms of tuxedos. Under the name of the store it said, "Established 1967."

"Wow, almost fifty years in business," Pickett said as they climbed out and headed through the warm afternoon air toward the front door. "That's downright ancient for this town."

"Family business," Sarge said, "if I remember right. Let me lead on this one. I have an idea."

"Be my guest," Pickett said, smiling at him as he once again held the door open for her. A girl could get used to that kind of treatment.

Inside the place was cool and bright, with racks of tuxedos along three walls and a lot of them on mannequins in different poses.

A man about their age came forward, smiling. "Can I be of service?"

The man had dark blue eyes and a smile that didn't reach his eyes. He was perfectly dressed in dark slacks and a tan shirt and matching tie. His gray hair was combed back, also perfectly.

"Detectives Carson and Pickett," Sarge said. "Would it be possible to ask you or one of the owners a few questions?"

Now the smile actually reached the man's eyes as he said, "I'm August LaPine, the owner. Be glad to answer what I can."

LaPine shook both of their hands in a formal manner and then led them to a counter in the back. LaPine went around the counter and then again smiled.

The counter was a display for all sorts of things like cufflinks and tie clasps and behind the counter were two desks, both neat, yet clearly used with new computers on both. This most certainly looked like a solid, well-run business.

"We're working on the Trudy Patterson case from 2010," Sarge said as Pickett watched LaPine.

The man showed no signs of awareness of the name in the slightest.

"Trudy was in town for her wedding and disappeared and was found dead about five days later. One of her stops that day was supposed to be here to check on the tuxes for her future husband and his friends."

"Oh, the poor girl. What day was that?" LaPine asked.

"May 17$^{th}$, 2010," Sarge said.

LaPine indicated they should wait a moment and he went to one desk and sat down and started working on a computer. A moment later LaPine nodded, hit a print button, waited for a moment for a paper to print, and then came back to the counter.

Pickett was impressed at how willing he was to help and how clearly organized his records were. But all the smiles and help seemed slightly fake and that bothered Sarge a little. Not sure why, but he made a note of it.

LaPine slid the paper around for the detectives to see. "She did reserve and pay half-down for the tuxedos. She never picked them up, so as per contract we kept her deposit. I have a note that a Detective Carson stopped by a week later to ask about her."

"I did," Sarge said, nodding. "So I was wondering, if it wouldn't be too much trouble, approximately how many no-shows like her do you have in a month?"

"A great deal," LaPine said, shaking his head, clearly seeming to be sad about the fact. "It's why we must ask for half down."

"Do you ever hear why some don't show?" Sarge asked. "Do they ever call in?"

"A few do," LaPine said, nodding. "If they give us enough notice, even though we don't have to, we refund their deposit. But most don't bother."

Pickett was impressed at where this was going. Not sure how it was going to help, but Sarge clearly had something on his mind.

"Say if you did a hundred reservations for tuxedos for weddings," Sarge said, "approximately how many wouldn't show without calling?"

"Ten or so," LaPine said. "Nature of the wedding business in Las Vegas I'm afraid."

"And you keep track of all the no-shows?" Sarge asked.

"We do," LaPine said, nodding.

"Thank you for your time," Sarge said, surprising Pickett as he stuck out his hand to shake LaPine's hand. "We're just doing some basic research to try to understand the wedding business in this town."

"Glad to be of service, detectives," LaPine said, bowing slightly as he shook Pickett's hand again.

With that, Sarge turned and headed for the front door and Pickett stayed with him.

When they reached the car and climbed in, Pickett turned to Sarge. "Want to explain what that was all about?"

Sarge smiled at her as she got the car started and the air-conditioning going.

"We need some more data. And as I remembered, that store is, and always has been, very organized."

"But we have no grounds to get a warrant for their files," Pickett said. Then the moment she said that, she laughed. "You know a guy who knows a guy, don't you?"

"We're only going to use the information for deep background," Sarge said, smiling at her. "LaPine will never know it's been borrowed. I'm just trying to figure out a way to narrow this mess down some."

Pickett just sat there smiling at the handsome man beside her.

"Lunch?" Sarge said.

"My stomach was thinking the same thing," Pickett said. "Bellagio Café is good and we're right out here."

"Perfect," Sarge said. "Want to have Robin join us?"

"We'll call her when we get there and see," Pickett said. She didn't say that waiting to call Robin until then would give her more time alone with Sarge and she wanted to get to know him better.

"Sounds great," Sarge said.

"Scares me how we think alike at times," Pickett said, finally moving and getting the car headed back toward the street.

"I kind of like it," Sarge said, smiling at her.

"Yeah, actually," Pickett said, "So do I."

And then she couldn't believe she had actually said that.

# CHAPTER TWELVE

*October 19th, 2016*
*Las Vegas, Nevada*

The Bellagio Café had an atmosphere Sarge really liked. Brown tones of oak and cloth, with lots of plants between the booths to give each booth a sense of privacy.

The sounds of the casino were muted and even the sound of others talking didn't seem to get very loud.

He often came here for lunch or dinner when out this far along the Strip. Almost always alone. His condo was far, far closer to the Golden Nugget than here, but this was his second favorite place.

One of the big reasons was that not only was it comfortable, but the food was good and the selection amazing at any time of the day or night.

He knew that Julia and Lott and Andor also came out here a great deal, but he didn't see them today, which he was glad about, actually. He really wanted to just spend a little time with Pickett to get to know her better.

Sarge waited until they got seated in a back booth before calling his friend Mike Dans while Pickett called Robin.

Mike and his girlfriend, Heather Voight often worked with Julia and Lott on cases as well. Sarge had met Mike on a robbery case about ten years before and liked him. Mike was a former Special Forces guy who hadn't lost a step or a bit of muscle. He kept his hair short and had an infectious smile that hid a brilliant mind.

He also controlled a small army of Special Forces retired soldiers for all sorts of jobs, many off the books.

Mike had done Sarge favors at times over the years and Sarge had done a few in return. Mike ran a security firm, only not a famous one like Robin's husband's firm, but a firm that stayed behind the scenes.

Mike and his people were also experts in all sorts of computer issues.

Mike sounded happy to hear from Sarge and was pleased to hear Sarge was back working again with the Cold Poker Gang.

Sarge quickly told Mike about the case they were working on, that it might be huge, and what he was thinking about the August Tux Shop records and how it might help them cross-reference a few details. And that no one would know and the records would only be used for deep background.

Mike seemed to have no issue with the favor and said he would e-mail Sarge the files that night.

As Sarge clicked off his phone, Pickett clicked off her phone as well.

"Robin will be here in thirty minutes," Pickett said. "She's bringing some information."

"My friend is getting us the August Tux Shop records tonight," Sarge said.

"Is this the same friend that works behind the scenes with Julia and Lott at times?" Pickett asked, smiling.

"One and the same," Sarge said.

"Got to meet this guy someday," Pickett said, shaking her head.

"I would think that with Robin and her husband's business," Sarge said, "you wouldn't need my friend."

"Oh, we need him," Pickett said, laughing. "For things like the reason you called him. Robin's people could never do that. Wouldn't dare."

"Then I'll be glad to introduce you when we get a chance," Sarge said, smiling.

They both ordered coffee and water and then Sarge decided he needed a snack while waiting for Robin, so he ordered them some chips and salsa.

After the waitress moved away, Sarge turned to face Pickett. She had scooted to the back of the booth to leave room for Robin. Sarge liked being that close to Pickett. It felt right and that should be worrying him, but it wasn't.

"So why did you retire?" Sarge asked. That seemed like the easiest question to start with to try to get to know her better.

Pickett smiled and stared at him with her wonderful brown eyes. "Honestly, both Robin and I were tired of the grind. Tired of the paperwork, and tired of being submerged in the cesspool of the lowlife of this city."

Sarge just nodded to that. "I know that feeling."

"After the ex ran off with his bimbo girlfriend," Pickett said, twisting her coffee cup in her hands, "I had enough money to do what I wanted, so figured I would do some traveling."

"Did you?" Sarge asked.

Pickett shrugged. "Don't much like hotel rooms considering all the crime scenes I saw in hotels here. And I would be away from Vegas for a few days and get bored and miss this stupid town."

Sarge laughed. "Wow, we really do think alike. I felt exactly the same way. Exactly."

"How much did you travel?" Pickett asked.

"The worst was a ten-day cruise," Sarge said. "All alone, bored out of my mind, and I couldn't eat enough or drink enough to change that, so I ended up reading a couple dozen novels. That I enjoyed."

"Robin and I were going to try that," Pickett said, shaking her head. "Came to our senses before it cost us too much."

Sarge decided to just plow on ahead. "Are you seeing anyone. None of my business, I know, but figured I would ask."

Pickett's brown eyes lit up and she smiled. "Nope. And you?"

"Nope," Sarge said. "Been thinking of getting a cat though."

Pickett actually laughed at that. "Can I help you pick it out? The shelters around here are always looking to find homes for some of the cats. I would love to help you rescue a few from the cages."

"You like cats?" Sarge said, actually surprised.

"Had one named Vice, but he died a couple of months before the ex left town with the bimbo. Haven't felt settled enough since to go for another."

"I love the name," Sarge said. "My wife and I had two named Come and Go. But they were her cats and she took them with her when she moved to Chicago. I missed the cats more than I missed her, which is kind of sad to say."

Pickett shook her head. "You know there is a horrid joke there about two cats named Come and Go leaving?"

"Oh, yeah," Sarge said. "And thanks for the restraint."

Picket laughed. Then said, "Feels empty at home, doesn't it?"

Sarge nodded. "And a goldfish just wouldn't do it."

Pickett laughed. "Then a cat it is."

"And I would love the help finding one."

"Deal," Pickett said.

At that moment their waitress came back with the chips and salsa and their coffees.

Sarge just smiled at Pickett as she dug into the chips. Damn he was starting to really be attracted to this woman.

He just hoped she felt the same. But only time was going to tell on that. Now at least he had help finding a cat or maybe two.

# CHAPTER THIRTEEN

*October 19th, 2016*
*Las Vegas, Nevada*

Robin joined them just a few minutes after the chips and salsa arrived. Pickett was very much enjoying the conversation with Sarge. Not only was he handsome, he wasn't seeing anyone, and he liked cats.

And he made her laugh. She hadn't laughed much in a very long time, so that felt great.

He felt a little too perfect, but at this point, at her age, she wasn't going to question too much an almost-mister-perfect. She was just going to enjoy her time with him and see what happened.

But she had to admit, after less than a day of knowing him, she was hoping a lot would happen between them.

Robin sat down, putting a couple of folders off to one side and dug into the chips as Sarge told Robin about the list of names they were getting from the August Tux Shop.

Robin just shook her head. "I didn't hear that," she said, "but I'm glad we are getting the records. They should help some."

"That bad?" Pickett asked. She knew the sound of her partner's voice and Robin sounded discouraged right now.

"Massive numbers," Robin said, opening a manila folder in front of her.

Pickett glanced at Sarge, who looked suddenly very worried.

"We dug only back to Trudy Patterson's disappearance in 2010," Robin said. "In a quick search, we found in six years over six thousand missing person's cases filed, men and women that had something to do with a marriage. That's out of the five hundred or more missing persons cases filed every month."

"Oh, wow," Pickett said. That sounded like an impossible number.

"We were able to eliminate just about half of those we targeted because the person actually was just running away from the marriage, either before or after, and showed up at home or called in when they discovered a report had been filed about them."

"That leaves three thousand in six years," Sarge said. "All attached to marriages, right?"

Robin nodded. "We eliminated another five hundred because of drunk marriages and one party or the other woke up and ran."

"Walk of shame with a marriage attached," Sarge said. "The worst kind."

Both Pickett and Robin laughed. Pickett was really starting to enjoy Sarge's sense of humor. He had a way of cutting building tension and keeping them focused.

"We got rid of another thousand," Robin said, "because the

couple was reported missing by family members, mostly parents of the bride."

"And they never showed up later?" Pickett asked.

"We never went any farther with those," Robin said. "And since missing person cases are never investigated unless there are suspicious circumstances, those had little information attached."

"So that leaves about fifteen hundred over six years," Sarge said.

Robin nodded. "Not quite one per week for the entire six years. All somehow attached to weddings. All now officially missing persons' cold cases."

"That many, huh?" Pickett asked. That number shocked her. She knew there were a lot of missing person cases in Vegas, but to hear it put that way was hard to grasp.

"I learned a ton about that side of our job today," Robin said. "The detectives that work missing persons are an amazing bunch in every precinct. And Las Vegas is the only city in the country at the moment to have a dedicated missing persons' cold case detective."

"You're kidding?" Pickett asked.

"Nope," Robin said. "We never met him. Started the job after we all retired. He works out of the main offices. And the missing person detectives around town use a lot of volunteers from the VIPS Program."

"What's that?" Sarge asked a half second before Pickett did.

"Volunteers in Police Service," Robin said. "We were really sheltered on the homicide side of things because volunteers were the last people we wanted messing around in a case. But with missing persons, quick action and lots of boots on the ground can often save lives."

"Wow," Sarge said, shaking his head. "Never knew."

Pickett shook her head as well.

"Lot of this is new, coming in about the time we three were calling it quits," Robin said. "There is now NCMA, the National Center for Missing Adults. We searched all their data bases as well this afternoon, plus a bunch more."

Pickett just looked at Sarge. For the first time in a while she was feeling in over her head on something, and from the look on Sarge's face, he wasn't feeling much different.

"So here is what my husband's people are doing," Robin said. "They are trying to file down that list by data-mining every database they can find around the world. Comparing everything from DNA to fingerprints to blood types and so on."

"Looking through morgue records as well?" Sarge asked.

"First place they are looking," Robin said. "Homicide cases, everything."

"So they might be able to get the number down to one per week since Trudy Patterson went missing and turned up dead," Sarge said.

Robin nodded. "If we're lucky."

Pickett stared at her partner, who was studying the file in front of her, then at Sarge, who seemed to be lost in thought.

"We also need to focus on the women who were falsely married, raped, and then let go," Pickett said.

Robin took a deep breath and Pickett didn't like that at all. Robin only did that when she had really bad news.

"About one per week," Robin said, "over the same time period, if you figure a certain normal percentage were never reported."

"Please tell me that number isn't certain," Sarge said.

Pickett just wanted to be sick.

"As close as we can figure it from the records," Robin said. "We figured that about a quarter of the cases would not be reported. Maybe more. That's why the August Tux Shop records will help us firm that up some."

Sarge sat back for a moment.

Robin went back to staring at the folder in front of her.

Pickett wanted to just toss this entire thing in and run away. Women abducted and raped right before getting married. The same number of women and men vanishing right before getting married. This was just too ugly to even try to wrap her mind around. As it was, she had no doubt she wouldn't be sleeping well over the next few nights. Something major was going on and regularly for a lot of years.

Sarge sat forward suddenly and looked at Robin. "Witnesses to the abductions? If these numbers are correct, we are having men and women abducted off Las Vegas streets at the pace of two per week. Someone has got to have seen something. Can we put the witness descriptions together to make a pattern?"

Robin shook her head. "So far we haven't found a single witness to an abduction in any of these cases."

"Nothing?" Pickett asked, now feeling even sicker.

"Nothing," Robin said. "The victims are just vanishing without a trace and the ones that come back from the rape have no memories."

"We'll," Sarge said, sitting back again and shaking his head. "That settles it."

Pickett looked at the handsome detective. "Settles what?"

"It's aliens," Sarge said. "Aliens in spaceships came and beamed them all up."

It took Pickett a moment to see the slight grin on Sarge's face before she and Robin both broke into laughter, breaking the tension of the moment.

But it was sad that the situation seemed so hopeless, alien abduction sounded plausible.

# THE PROBLEM GETS BIGGER

# CHAPTER FOURTEEN

*October 19th, 2016*
*Las Vegas, Nevada*

Sarge and Pickett and Robin spent the rest of their lunch at the Bellagio Café working to figure out where to start into all this. And what they came back around to was focusing on Trudy Patterson's abduction and then death.

But at the same time, Robin would continue looking for patterns among the fifteen hundred that had gone missing around their own future wedding and stayed missing. And also look for patterns in the rape cases focused also on marriages.

Around them the normal world went on with the distant sounds of the casino and other lunch customers eating and laughing. Sarge bet most of the people near them would be appalled at what the three of them had been talking about so casually.

It was right at the end of lunch, when Robin was about to head back to her computer people, that Sarge had one more idea. He didn't much like the idea, but it seemed logical to at least add it in.

"We're dealing in three different areas of detective work," Sarge said. "Missing persons, sexual assault, and homicide. Right?"

Pickett looked at him with a puzzled look and nodded.

"So how many unsolved homicide cases do we have similar to Trudy Patterson's case that had a future wedding in the mix?"

Robin flipped back open her notebook that she had closed and started writing.

"Good thought," Pickett said, nodding.

"A little more in our wheelhouse, at least," Sarge said.

At that point Robin closed her book and scooted out of the booth. "I'm headed back to the computer elves. We got a lot of information to crunch to pull some patterns."

Sarge watched her go and then glanced at Pickett. "She always leave that suddenly?"

"Always," Pickett said, laughing, "when she's focused on a case."

"So any idea how we figure out how these women and men are being targeted?" Sarge asked, sipping on the last of his coffee. He had almost finished his club sandwich before finally pushing it away for the waitress to take. After that much food, coffee tasted wonderful.

"I had a thought after we talked with Stein," Pickett said. "These couples will have a bridal registry for gifts. That has an outside chance of being a link and I mentioned it to Robin."

"I wouldn't even begin to know how those work," Sarge said. "Are the gifts picked out and bought delivered to the chapel or hotel room or something? Or just brought by the people who bought them?"

"Yes," Pickett said, smiling.

Damn he was coming to really enjoy her smile. And she had the whitest teeth he had seen in a long time, especially for a detective who drank a lot of coffee.

"The problem with bridal registry is that not many do it these days," Pickett said, "and gifts are often just sent to their homes. So after I had that thought and talked with Robin, we have pretty much ruled it out."

Sarge smiled. "I do that all the time. Come up with an idea and then talk myself away from it. At least on this case that is considered progress."

"Agreed," Pickett said. "So we need to really figure out how these women and men are being targeted. There has to be one point all of them walk through."

Sarge instantly knew where that was. "County clerk is the only common thing they all do ahead of time."

Pickett nodded. "They must show proof of identity to pick up their license."

Sarge quickly picked up his phone and called Mike Dans.

"Still early," Mike said.

"This is another lead," Sarge said, smiling at Pickett who looked a little puzzled. "Would it be possible for you to check, very, very carefully, to see if a system database has been hacked?"

Pickett smiled and nodded, now understanding what he was doing.

"Sure," Mike said. "Which one are we talking about?"

"County clerk's office for marriage licenses," Sarge said. "At this point, until we get more data, it's the only place we know for sure every person touched who disappeared or was raped or murdered with a wedding in their future."

"Ahh," Mike said. "Damn good thinking. It shouldn't take

too long to carefully see if there was a hack without setting off alarms. Back with you in ten minutes."

"Thanks," Sarge said, and clicked off his phone.

He turned to Pickett. "Figured we had better determine if there was a hack from the outside before digging into the county employees."

"A really, really good idea," Pickett said. "How long until he can figure it out?"

"Ten minutes," Sarge said.

"He's that fast?" Pickett asked, clearly shocked.

"He's that good," Sarge said, grinning. "He'll go in and leave no trace or set off any alarm a hacker might have installed."

"Damn," Pickett said. "We turn over enough rocks, we might actually find a slug."

"You believe that?" Sarge asked, smiling.

"Nope," Pickett said. "Not with this case. But a girl can hope."

"I like hope," Sarge said, laughing. "And some luck might be nice here as well."

Pickett's beautiful face suddenly became very serious. "I have another rock we really need to turn over."

Sarge looked at her and nodded for her to go on.

"If this is all tied together," Pickett said, "which it sure seems like it might be, I think we need to focus on what kind of person could be doing this."

Sarge sat back in the booth, thinking. Pickett was right. They hadn't given any thought at all to the type of person, or group of people who could do these crimes. And do them so perfectly as to not have even one witness in six years.

"And why?" he said, looking at her. "If fifteen hundred people have vanished right before their weddings, where did they go?"

"And why release some and not others," Pickett asked.

"Assuming this is all tied together," Sarge said.

"Yeah, assuming that."

Sarge had no doubt that it all was tied together. And until now, no one had put the entire picture together before because of the vast size of the wedding industry in Las Vegas.

And that worried him more than he wanted to admit.

# CHAPTER FIFTEEN

*October 19th, 2016*
*Las Vegas, Nevada*

Pickett let the soothing sounds of the restaurant and casino wash over her as she sipped on her coffee and thought about the problem of profiling the person or people doing this.

She knew they were making an assumption that all of this was tied together, but it was the only assumption she felt comfortable with at this point.

It seemed unlikely that fifteen hundred people could go missing before weddings and never be found in such a short amount of time. Sure, thousands went missing all the time in Vegas, but they could account for most of those now over the last six years.

And they knew that the rapes were tied together because of the exact same circumstances of each one.

So it wasn't that far of a leap to tie the missing persons with the rapes. They just needed to figure out why some victims were handled differently.

"I might have someone who could help us with the profiling," Sarge said after a moment when they both sat sipping their coffee. "We'll check him out this afternoon, see if he'll help us, but I have another question that might help Robin do some connections."

Pickett stared into the handsome face of the detective sitting beside her in the booth. In less than one day she had become amazingly comfortable being beside him and talking with him.

And she flat loved looking into his hazel eyes. At this point his face was puzzled and very serious, which made him even more handsome.

Pickett managed to nod and look down at her coffee before she did something like a young school girl.

"Rental cars," Sarge said.

Pickett instantly looked back into his eyes. "What are you thinking?"

Sarge shrugged. "Wondering if there is a pattern with rental cars. They are hard to ditch and easy to track."

Pickett was stunned at the very idea. "Are you thinking that maybe if the victim was driving a rental car, they were raped and put back in their car, but if driving an owned car, they were taken?"

"Grasping at straws," he said, shaking his head. "Said out loud like that, it sounds even crazier than it sounded in my head."

"This might be more like a fire hose if you are right," Pickett said, grabbing her phone and calling Robin.

"Sarge has an idea," Pickett said before Robin could even say hello. "Can you check and see if only the rape victims had rental cars and the missing people had regular cars when they were taken?"

"Shit," Robin said. "Give me thirty minutes. My husband has given me two more people to help on the computers on this. He thinks we may be on to something huge here and wants his best helping us nail it down."

"Wonderful," Pickett said.

That made her feel even better about the assumption this was tied together if Will and Robin both had the same feeling.

Robin hung up and Picket clicked off her phone and smiled at Sarge. "Thirty minutes."

Sarge indicated to a passing waitress that they both needed fresh coffee. Then he said, "Now this is the kind of detective work I like. Sitting and drinking coffee and coming up with ideas while others do the work."

Pickett laughed and let the waitress fill her cup. She had no doubt this was about as far from standard detective work that Sarge got. But she had to admit, for the moment this did feel great.

Especially sitting beside him.

# CHAPTER SIXTEEN

*October 19th, 2016*
*Las Vegas, Nevada*

Mike called Sarge back after a couple more minutes and about half-a-cup of coffee.

"It's hacked," Mike said without even a hello. "A good one, downloading full data twice a month in a flash grab. It had alarms all over it to go off and erase itself if found."

"Shit," Sarge said. "I was afraid of that. Traceable?"

"We're working on that," Mike said, "but chances are, from the level of the sophistication on this, it's going to a dark web location, not traceable and not in existence for more than a few seconds that this hack takes every couple of weeks."

"How long has it been going on?" Sarge asked. He didn't really want to know the answer, but he had to.

"Best we can figure, it started in early 2008."

Sarge felt his stomach just tighten into a knot. Over eight

years this had been going on without anyone having a clue. How was that possible?

"Thanks, Mike. I owe you," Sarge said. "Now at least we know how these sickos are finding the victims."

"I'll keep my people on this and see if we can trace it and feed them old data on the next hack, which will be in ten days. You still need the data from the tux place?"

"Skip it," Sarge said. "I think we got enough."

"Figured," Mike said. "I'll be back to you when I got more."

Mike clicked off and Sarge slowly lowered his phone and put it on the table in front of him.

"That bad, huh?" Pickett asked.

Sarge glanced at her very worried face. Her eyes seemed to be almost slits and her mouth was tight and firm.

Sarge nodded. "Mike found a very sophisticated hack on the County Clerk's records for marriage certificates."

Pickett sat back, clearly stunned.

"The records are hacked twice a month and it has been going on since early 2008. He's trying to trace it, but doubt it will work. We got ten days until the next one and Mike's going to try to feed the hack false data at that point."

"We need to extend back the search two years ahead of Trudy Patterson," Pickett said, her voice hushed and soft. "That's a lot of people."

All Sarge could do was nod. His nightmare case had turned into a complete horror, not only for poor Trudy Patterson, but for a lot of other men and women.

Pickett quickly called Robin and told her what they had discovered and to extend the pattern searches back to 2008.

"We need to keep this to ourselves for the moment," Pickett said to Robin. "Swear your husband to secrecy even with top officials, because if this gets leaked, it might spook these sickos.

We don't know who they are and we only have ten days until the next hack."

Pickett nodded for a moment, then said, "Will do."

After she clicked off her phone, Sarge asked, "Will do what?"

"Be careful," Pickett said. "This is a lot bigger than one cold case."

Sarge could only nod at that.

They sat, not talking, both thinking, as the happy, real world of the surface of Las Vegas went on around them. Dishes clicking, people laughing, the sounds of slot machines announcing a winner.

But there was so much more under the surface in this town.

So much happened the tourists here for a good time just didn't see. He always knew that as a detective, but something about the size, scale, and focus on the happy moments of a wedding really made him even more disgusted at his own city.

But as long as the tourists didn't know or care, things were fine.

And that was just better for everyone concerned.

# CHAPTER SEVENTEEN

*October 19th, 2016*
*Las Vegas, Nevada*

Pickett was now certain that all the disappearances and rapes were tied together. And she was betting there were very few homicides besides Trudy Patterson's death attached. She just had that feeling.

So now they had options. None of them good, but they had options.

"So let's say over the last six years," Pickett said to Sarge, "since Trudy Patterson was taken, about two thousand others were taken and fifteen hundred of them disappeared completely while five hundred of the women were raped and released. How is something like that possible in a town with a million security cameras?"

Sarge turned to face her, nodding. "We have in the file security footage of Trudy Patterson leaving the parking garage of her hotel but nothing after that."

"When did rental car companies start putting in tracking devices for their cars?"

"Worth figuring out," Sarge said. "If we know these cases are linked, we should be able to find patterns in how the people were abducted."

"Exactly what I was thinking," Pickett said. "In this case numbers work on our side. I am sure that Robin and Will and their people are already on that part of things."

"So how about we tackle the why?" Sarge asked.

"Why would a group of people kidnap that many people?" Pickett asked. "First thing that springs to mind is the sex slave trade. The victims are being sold overseas."

She hated the idea, but it was the most logical from where they were sitting. But the wedding part made no sense at all with that.

Sarge looked at her. "You think it is the sex slave trade?"

"I hope not," Pickett said.

"Either way," Sarge said, nodding, "You think any of these missing are still alive?"

"I can't imagine how or why?" Pickett said. And she couldn't. After this many years, it would be logical that if the missing were kept alive, one or two would get away and return, even from sex slave trafficking. It did happen.

"So we go on the theory we have a real sicko serial rapist and killer," Sarge said. "Let's go see if we can get some profiling help on this while Robin does her magic."

Pickett nodded as Sarge stood from the booth and tossed enough money on the bill to cover it and a good tip.

"Next time my turn to buy," Pickett said.

He smiled. "Deal. But I didn't tell you I have enough money to last me far longer than I'm going to live. Family inheritance four years ago. Father died, I was the only child and he was disgustingly rich."

Now she understood why he had quit the Cold Poker Gang the first time. He had been dealing with that.

"That rich, huh?" Pickett said.

"Triple disgustingly, actually," Sarge said, laughing.

At that he indicated they should head out of the restaurant and deeper into the casino. Even with the wide aisles, the number of people and families kept them both weaving in and out of tourists.

The Bellagio poker room was a beautiful room off to one side of a slot machine area. It was decorated in ornate oak wood and rich furnishings and from what she could tell a good dozen tables were full of players.

Sarge indicated she should stay outside for a moment and he went inside and up a few steps in the back to a slightly higher level to a game going on inside a glassed-in room off the back. Pickett bet that was a high-stakes game. The Bellagio was known for that.

She watched as Sarge stood outside the room for a moment until a man inside smiled and stood and headed to the door. The man was about thirty and tall and rugged and had a tan that surprised Pickett even for the sun of Las Vegas. He wore a dress shirt with the sleeves rolled up and jeans and tennis shoes. She recognized him from somewhere, but she couldn't remember where.

Sarge and the man came across the poker room and out to where she stood to one side of the flow of tourists. Around her the sounds of the slot machines filled the air, but not so much as to make it impossible to hold a decent conversation.

"Detective Pickett," Sarge said, "I'd like you to meet Doc Hill."

Pickett shook Doc's hand, nodding. "Annie's boyfriend, Lott's daughter. Right?"

Doc smiled a smile that could melt ice from a hundred yards. "Guilty as charged."

"Wonderful to meet you," Pickett said. She was now also remembering that she had seen Doc's picture on a number of magazines over the last few years. And that he was amazingly rich and helped out Lott and Julia and Andor with cases all the time, sort of in the same way that Will helped out her and Robin with cases.

"So what can I do for you, detectives?" Doc asked.

"We're working on a really ugly case that is seeming to explode in size around us," Sarge said. "And we're looking for some profiling help on who might be pulling the strings. Thinking maybe Mac might help, but I don't know him well enough to ask."

Doc nodded and glanced around at the room behind him. Pickett had no idea who Sarge was talking about, but Doc seemed to think the idea made sense.

"I'll get him," Doc said. "Looks like he could use a break."

Doc turned and headed back into the poker room.

"Mac used to be an FBI profiler," Sarge said, "one of the best in the business, before going to play poker full time. He can read a person sitting across from him with the best players in the business and has gotten rich using his skills on other poker players."

Pickett nodded. That sounded like the best hope they had at the moment to even start to get inside this case.

She watched as Doc knelt down beside a guy with a gray cap clearly covering a bald head.

The guy listened to Doc for a moment, then said something

to the table and stood with Doc. Both of them turned toward the door to the room.

Mac couldn't have been any taller than five-five and was a distance beyond two hundred pounds. Pickett guessed him to be in his early forties. He had on dark dress slacks and a white long-sleeved shirt with the cuffs buttoned.

Doc introduced them, then said, "I'm going to get back."

"Thanks, Doc," Sarge said.

"Thanks for the break," Mac said to them after Doc left. "I was grinding and getting hungry, not a good state to be in while playing poker with the likes of the sharks at that table."

"Doc said you looked like you could use a break," Pickett said, smiling.

"That guy scares me sometimes," Mac said, shaking his head.

"Cheeseburger and fries for a half hour of your time?" Sarge asked, smiling.

Mac smiled at Pickett and winked. "Detectives, you toss in a milkshake and you can have thirty-five minutes."

"Deal," Sarge said, laughing.

And back they went toward the Bellagio Café.

Pickett had no doubt she was going to spend far more time than she normally did in the café before this case was all over.

# CHAPTER EIGHTEEN

*October 19th, 2016*
*Las Vegas, Nevada*

They got settled back in the same booth Sarge and Pickett had just left. It had been cleaned off and Mac took Robin's spot.

Sarge wasn't sure what he was going to ask Mac, but figured this was worth a shot.

Pickett got out a notebook and Sarge took his small notebook out of his pocket as the waitress took their drink orders and the order for Mac's meal.

Sarge ordered himself and Pickett a basket of fries to share since it seemed wrong to not eat while Mac did.

"You do know," Mac said after the waitress left, "that anything I can tell you here about your case is just going to be off-the-cuff opinion. To do what I used to do right would take a lot of detail work and time and more information than you are going to be able to give me."

Sarge and Pickett both nodded.

"Actually," Sarge said, "even an opinion will put us farther along than we are."

"That bad, huh?" Mac asked.

"Worse," Pickett said.

"So lay it out for me," Mac said.

He pulled out a small notebook from his back pocket and a pen from his shirt pocket and opened to a blank page.

Sarge glanced at Pickett and she nodded that he tell Mac the case.

In five minutes, Sarge told Mac about Trudy Patterson and how that started all this, the information about the rapes, the fact that the wedding license information was hacked twice a month with a very sophisticated hack, and that somehow over 1,500 people had vanished completely from Las Vegas without a trace right before the weddings over the last six to eight years.

Mac wrote down notes, shaking his head at times. Finally, when Sarge was done, Mac looked up. Sarge could see the man's eyes were haunted.

"That bad, huh?" Sarge asked.

"As bad as you think it is," Mac said. "The wedding is the key. You are on the right track there, I have no doubt."

"We just can't find a damn door any key fits yet," Pickett said.

"Weddings are a marker of a new beginning," Mac said. "Crossing into a new life. That symbolism is powerful, if not real for the perps here."

Sarge sat back. "Starting over?"

Mac nodded. "Starting over. And to the perps something is flawed with the women who are raped and released. Something about them doesn't fit what the perps are looking for so they use them for something else."

"We were thinking they might have had rental cars and the others didn't," Sarge said.

Mac shook his head. "It's something far more personal than that. I would run the details about the women who were raped, see if any one thing comes up that makes them similar in some fashion and unacceptable."

Sarge looked at Pickett who was frowning. "We need to have Mike search the women's medical records."

"Mike Dans?" Mac asked.

Sarge nodded.

"Mike would do it right," Mac said. "Good idea. But also interview a few of them, look through their records, rape kits, things like that to see if you can find a pattern."

Sarge looked at Pickett who was writing in her notebook and nodding. That was going to be a lot more work for Robin, but Sarge had a hunch she and her husband's team could handle it, if they weren't already doing it.

At that moment their food came and Mac dug into his cheeseburger.

Sarge sort of pretended to take a fry, but he wasn't hungry in the slightest, even though they smelled great.

Pickett put down her pen and grabbed the salt shaker. "Mind?" she asked.

"Please," Sarge said and Pickett salted the fries about as much as Sarge would have.

"So any opinions from what little we know what these sickos are like?" Pickett asked Mac.

"Controlling," Mac said between bites. "Of that there is no doubt. Very careful, very meticulous, very sexual focused."

"Slave trade?" Sarge asked.

Mac shook his head. "I doubt it with the marriage connection. I dealt with my share of those who kidnapped for the sex trades and this doesn't have that feel."

Sarge wasn't sure if he was relieved or disappointed.

"Marriage often has a religious element to it," Mac said. "So chances are these people are religious which is why they are marrying the victims of the rapes before the sexual act."

Sarge and Pickett both nodded and Pickett wrote it down in her notebook. All of what Mac was saying made sense so far.

"If I could make one more bet on this," Mac said. "I would bet the people involved have a lot of money and are possibly community leaders. Going on this long without even a crack in the pattern is a sign of money, intelligence, and connections. So be careful who you talk to."

And with that, Mac finally said something that just scared hell out of Sarge.

And Sarge had a hunch Mac was right.

# CHAPTER NINETEEN

*October 19th, 2016*
*Las Vegas, Nevada*

Pickett and Sarge walked Mac back to the poker room and thanked him again.

"Keep me in the loop if I can help," Mac said.

Pickett promised him they would, and then she and Sarge headed back for her car.

She had no idea what they were going to do next. Not an idea, but clearly they both felt they needed to be moving doing something.

Robin and Will were both still working at all the data, trying to pull any pattern that would help them pry open a door with this thing. And that was going to take a little more time, if not all night and into tomorrow to even dent the vast size and scope of all this.

Pickett walked beside Sarge in silence out the door and

across the parking lot. The day was warming, but not hot. It actually felt good to Pickett.

Sarge was clearly in as much thought about all this as she was, and the silence didn't feel uncomfortable at all. In fact, it felt as if they had been partners for years already.

She liked that.

And she really liked having Sarge at her side. It felt right and very comfortable. And she still hadn't known him for a full day yet.

As they got in and she got the SUV running and the climate controls set, she turned to him before putting on her seat belt. "Any ideas?"

"A couple," he said, nodding, looking straight ahead and clearly thinking.

She waited a moment until he was ready to put the ideas into words. Robin waited for her in the same way.

After just a few seconds, Sarge turned slightly in his seat to face her. "I'm thinking there are two areas here where we might catch a break. First are the victims' cars. That's been haunting me."

"Rental cars are tracked all the time these days," Pickett said, nodding. "And some newer model cars as well."

Sarge nodded.

That same thing had been bothering her as well, but she honestly had no idea how they could get to the data if it wasn't already in the files for each case. And she couldn't imagine the rape detectives not following up on that with each victim. So Robin and Will would have some answers in that area, she hoped.

"So how do these people hide the cars from tracking?" Sarge said. "Or do they? Think Robin and Will might know that?"

"I would think that would be a major area she and Will and

her computer elves are digging into," Pickett said. "But if not, you might be able to get Mike Dans and his people really digging behind the scenes."

Sarge nodded, again staring straight ahead.

"But what about your second idea?" Pickett asked.

Sarge again turned and looked at her. "This doesn't feel like kidnapping for selling sex slaves overseas. But I can't seem to let go of the fact that both men and women have vanished. Why both? That shouts to me sex trade of some sort."

Pickett sat back, thinking. He was right.

But for what reason were both men and women taken?

"If this was any kind of sex trade," Sarge said, going on, "wouldn't there have been some reports of sightings of the missing people at some point."

"Maybe there have been," Pickett said. "I would hope those would have gotten to the files. We can check with Robin after they get more of this together."

"So you and Robin have any contacts that would know the sex trade in this city?" Sarge asked.

Pickett laughed. "Actually, we do."

Sarge looked at her and then smiled. "Don't tell me it's the former wife of Elvis with hair that won't fall down?"

"Then I won't tell you that," Pickett said, laughing. "But Stein knows a ton about everything to do with weddings and the underground scene of hookers and walkers and sexual fetishes."

"Hand-in-hand with weddings?" Sarge asked.

"It's huge business in this town to help with bachelor and bachelorette parties," Pickett said as she started up the car. "Bigger money than the weddings, actually."

"Of course," Sarge said, shaking his head and laughing as he buckled his seat belt. "Just not one of those connections I would make naturally."

Pickett laughed. "Didn't want to think about that part with your daughter, did you?"

"Have I told you how happy I was that she eloped to Hawaii?"

"You mentioned that," Pickett said, smiling at the handsome man in the seat beside her.

# CHAPTER TWENTY

*October 19th, 2016*
*Las Vegas, Nevada*

Sarge sat comfortably beside Pickett as she worked her Jeep SUV through traffic like an expert. He couldn't remember being so comfortable riding with someone before.

They were headed back to Stein's old wedding chapel. Sarge didn't consider himself a prude and after an entire career on the Las Vegas police force, he had seen most everything. But he had a hunch he just might learn a few new things this afternoon and the idea didn't excite him in the slightest.

About two blocks from the chapel, Robin called and Pickett put it on speaker.

"Sarge and I are headed to talk with Stein again," Pickett said. "What do you have?"

"A bunch of stuff starting to shape into patterns," Robin said.

Sarge sat forward, feeling a flush of excitement for the first time in this case.

"Hang on a sec," Pickett said. She swung across two lanes of traffic and into an empty parking lot and parked.

"I'm stopped," Pickett said. "Fire away."

"We've been going back and digging out information from the rental car companies on the rape victims who had them," Robin said. "The tracking all shuts off or is blocked in the same general area, a circle about ten blocks in diameter just off the Strip and to the west of the University."

"And turns back on?" Pickett asked a moment before Sarge could.

"When the car leaves the circle," Robin said.

"Blocking frequency," Sarge said. "That's a lot of territory inside that circle."

"Works with rape victims with modern cars and OnStar as well," Robin said.

"What's at the center of that circle?" Pickett asked. "Anything to do with weddings?"

"The August Tux Shop," Robin said.

"Shit, shit, shit," Sarge said. He wanted to punch something, including that bastard who owned the place.

"Not all victims and missing persons got near the tux shop," Robin said.

"I'm betting you discover with enough digging," Pickett said, "that the owner or owners of the tux shop also own other bridal and tux shops around town."

"You got it in one," Robin said. "But all cars vanish into that circle around the August Tux Shop. The missing people's cars never reappear."

"They don't?" Sarge asked. "There a garage near there?"

"Nothing at all close by," Robin said.

Sarge just shook his head. How in the world did fifteen hundred or more modern cars go missing in this new world?

"Well," Pickett said, "that's a ton more than we had before."

Sarge could only agree with that. This felt like a major step forward, all because of good computer work.

"We're still digging," Robin said. "Very, very carefully. The information on the hack on the clerk records really clamped a lid on our security and slowed us down a bunch."

"For the better," Pickett said.

"I agree," Sarge said. "Robin, on the missing persons cases, have there been sightings reported?"

"A couple dozen in the records is all," Robin said. "All in sex tapes that might have been done before the person vanished for all the detectives knew."

"Overseas type of stuff?" Pickett asked.

"No," Robin said. "All peeping tom voyeur crap. Hidden cameras. Faces not shown or blurred, but the people reporting them didn't want to say where they supposedly saw the person. You know the type. A friend of a friend saw this but there is no record and no one would admit to going to one of the porn sites."

Sarge looked at Robin who was looking puzzled.

"All the reports were like that?" Sarge asked.

"All the ones we have found so far that the detectives put into files," Robin said.

Sarge had a very large hunch that was a key, but damned if he knew how they could even begin to trace that. The underground porn world was huge and very secretive in the fetish areas. He knew that much.

"Keep looking in on that, would you?" Pickett said. "We'll ask Stein about it in a few minutes."

Robin laughed. "Anyone know about that kind of shit it

would be Stein, the queen of the porn wedding photographers. Let me know if you learn anything."

And then Robin clicked off.

"Porn wedding photographers?" Sarge asked Pickett as she got the car going again.

"This is Vegas," Robin said, laughing. "An amazing number of newlyweds want their first night recorded as well. Maybe show their kids or something when the couple gets fat and old."

Sarge just sat there looking at the traffic around him. He had been right. By the time this case was over, he was going to learn stuff he didn't really want to know.

Too much stuff.

# NOTHING IS AS IT SEEMS

# CHAPTER TWENTY-ONE

*October 19th, 2016*
*Las Vegas, Nevada*

Pickett thanked Sarge for holding open the large front door to Stein's chapel. Over the years, since Stein's husband had died, nothing had changed at all in here, except for the fact that once in a while someone emptied the ashtrays on the coffee tables. But it still smelled of old cigarettes and a faint smell of lilacs.

Stein came out of the back room, smiling as she always did. Her hair hadn't changed at all in years and Pickett couldn't imagine the work it took to keep that massive beehive on her head and in place. Either that or the beehive was fake, but Pickett and Robin over the years could never spot any sign of that. And they had both looked.

And neither of them had had the courage to ask.

"Detectives," Stein said. "Back so soon."

"Third time's the charm," Sarge said, smiling at Stein who just sort of beamed at the handsome detective.

"We're digging up more and more dirt," Pickett said. "Can you keep what we are about to talk about among the three of us?"

"Sure can," Stein said, and indicated that they should follow her.

She led them through a second room that clearly had been the wedding chapel at one point, but had now fallen into dust-covered relics. Clearly no customer came back this way and Pickett had never been in this area either in all the years of knowing Stein.

Stein led them into the back into a large office that was clean and well-organized. She indicated chairs and then closed the door behind them. A number of monitors showed that the entire building was under surveillance and Stein could see everything going on around the building from her office.

"I record everything in this building except what goes on in this office," Stein said, indicating the monitors as she closed the door and moved around behind her desk.

"Clients wanting to skip on agreements, huh?"

"That," Stein said, nodding, "and asking for things illegal that I don't provide. I don't mind a few kinks in the wedding planning, but I draw the line at illegal."

Pickett nodded and she could see out of the corner of her eye that Sarge was nodding as well.

"You're going to ask me to keep some secrets," Stein said. "I need you to keep one as well."

"No problem," Pickett said.

"Thanks," Stein said. "This damn thing is killing me today for some reason. Just couldn't get it to settle into place this morning."

With that she reached up and using both hands she pulled off all the hair on her head and set the beehive and the hair that looked like it had been on her scalp on the corner of her desk like a trophy.

Stein was impressed that it didn't move or fall over or even jiggle like a bowl of jelly.

Stein was completely bald and it actually looked good on her. She looked twenty years younger and far more alive, which surprised Pickett. She never would have recognized Stein on the street without the hair.

Stein then quickly took off the three pieces of tape that were stuck to her scalp and sighed. "That's better."

Sarge laughed and said, "I was wondering how you managed that miracle."

"As with most things in Vegas," Stein said, smiling at Sarge, "things are not always what they appear."

Pickett laughed as Sarge just shook his head and smiled.

"So what's going on?" Stein asked, leaning forward. "You two closing in on the Wedding Rapist?"

"Not closing in," Pickett said, "but finally getting a little traction. What can you tell us about the August Tux Shop?"

Pickett thought Stein was going to spit as she sat back. "Other than to avoid them at all costs, not much. They overcharge for everything and make all sorts of reasons to not do refunds when another place would."

"Anything else?" Sarge asked, making a note in his notebook.

"Family that owns the place is stupidly rich," Stein said. "And they didn't get it from overcharging for tuxes. Not sure where the money came from. Might be worth checking into, but careful, that family is just flat nasty."

Pickett nodded and waited a moment until Sarge finished writing in his small notebook, then she asked Stein the next question. "We've had a few reports about some missing persons who went missing right before their weddings who turned up in porn videos."

Stein shrugged. "No surprise. People seem to think others will find their humping attractive."

"These were all voyeur videos," Pickett said.

Stein actually showed surprise at that. "Are there enough of them to show a pattern?"

"Working on that," Pickett said. "Anything you can help us on that?"

Stein shook her head. "Filming someone without their permission in a private place is very, very damn illegal. Some of the grooms want me to do that on their wedding night and when I try to get the bride's permission, the wedding usually is suddenly called off."

Pickett laughed. "I wonder why?"

Stein just shook her head. "I've heard of a number of houses down near campus where college kids for free room and board and a little cash every month agree to be filmed twenty-four-seven."

Pickett nodded and she could see Sarge nodding beside her.

"Any money in that sort of thing?" Sarge asked.

"Porn is a billion dollar business," Stein said. "A lot of the money goes unreported. There is something out there catering to all kinds."

"Wedding porn?" Sarge asked.

Stein nodded. "Lots of young couples are here for free, making a nice killing and getting a free trip and wedding because they agreed with some company or another to be filmed on their wedding night. Of course, they have to film some of the wedding and she has to keep the dress on for a while in bed and it has to last a certain amount of time. I stay away from the couples doing it for the money."

"Never see their faces?" Sarge asked, glancing at Pickett, then back at Stein.

"Nah, never," Stein said. "Even the ones just into it for their own viewing pleasure don't want their faces in the mix."

Pickett sat back and again watched as Sarge wrote. But she had a hunch they might have just figured out why some women were married and then raped.

It was a hell of a lot cheaper to get actors that way than paying for a vacation and wedding.

# CHAPTER TWENTY-TWO

*October 19th, 2016*
*Las Vegas, Nevada*

Sarge listened twenty minutes later as they sat in Pickett's car and she filled Robin in on what they had discovered. And their theory on why the rapes had happened.

Sarge didn't much like the theory, but at the moment it fit both a reason why and also what Max had said about the type of people doing these crimes being focused on sex.

"We'll see if we can find a money trail leading into that tux shop business," Robin said.

Sarge doubted that would be possible with the porn industry, but it was worth the shot. At this point, any lead was worth a shot.

So when Pickett hung up and turned to him, he just shook his head. "So we add in more suppositions."

Pickett nodded. "And no real suspects on any of this."

"Besides the family behind the tux shop," Sarge said.

"Besides them," Pickett said, nodding. "More than we had I suppose."

They both sat quietly for a moment, then Sarge asked the question that had been bothering him from before going in to see Stein.

"We are working on where the people are going, but where are the cars going to?"

Pickett looked at him with those wonderful brown eyes. "You think something more is happening besides taking out the tracking and moving them?"

"Seems that there were police reports on many of those cars fairly quickly after the kidnappings," Sarge said, trying to make sense of what was bothering him. "It would be risky to move the cars if the person was disappearing for good."

"But that would mean about fifteen hundred or more cars over the years," Pickett said. "Where would you put them? There are no warehouses or shops at all in that blank tracking area."

"There is nowhere to put them," Sarge said, still not getting what his mind was trying to get to. "So they had to be moved. Maybe by truck, maybe after being painted and such."

"Or chopped up and sold for parts," Pickett said.

Sarge nodded, but he didn't feel that was right either. A shop or warehouse of that size could be seen in that area and there just wasn't one.

Again they sat there in silence. It was a comfortable silence, something Sarge really enjoyed, actually. He just hadn't felt this comfortable with another person in a very long time.

"Any ideas on where to go next?" Pickett asked.

"Not a one," Sarge said.

"So how about I drop you back at your car," Pickett said.

"I'd like to get some running in and clear my head some. I like running every afternoon in the exercise room in my building."

Sarge laughed. "Actually, I was thinking I could use a nap to try to clear my head a little as well, so sounds good."

"Don't you love this retirement stuff?" Pickett asked, smiling, as she got the car moving and headed back onto Las Vegas Boulevard. "Naps and exercise when we want."

"Beats the hell out of the paperwork," Sarge said, laughing.

"Got that right," Pickett said.

# CHAPTER TWENTY-THREE

*October 19th, 2016*
*Las Vegas, Nevada*

Pickett dropped Sarge back at the Golden Nugget parking garage and then headed back to her condo in the Ogden.

She was surprised at how instantly she missed having Sarge beside her. She hadn't felt that way about anyone for a very long time, and she had only known Sarge for just a day. Yet she felt completely comfortable beside him and liked having him around a lot more than she wanted to admit.

And besides all that, she found him amazingly handsome. She wasn't sure how all that combined could be possible.

She spent forty-five minutes putting in some miles on the treadmill and then took a quick shower. It didn't help her come up with any new ideas, but it made her feel better.

Two hours later, she was back at the Golden Nugget, this time in the steak house with the big fish tank in the center. Sarge was already there and Robin had called and said she would be twenty minutes late. Picket had to admit she didn't mind the alone time with Sarge at all.

Sarge looked even more handsome than earlier. He had on a light suit jacket with an open-collar blue shirt under it. His thick, gray hair was combed back and shaped his square face perfectly. She now felt glad she had decided to dress up a little.

Sarge had said he was buying dinner tonight. He said he had been looking for an excuse to try out the steak house here, but could never make himself go in alone.

Pickett had gladly agreed to help out with his test run of a new restaurant. The place had cloth tablecloths, cloth napkins, three empty glasses in front of each place, and a bunch of silverware including one fork turned sideways across the top of her clearly expensive plate. She never felt that comfortable in these sorts of high-end restaurants, but she had a hunch Sarge would ease that discomfort a lot.

He stood as she approached their table and pulled out her chair. She just shook her head. "Always a gentleman, huh?"

He laughed as they sat down. "I'm sure many people would call me far worse names than that."

"Why detective," she said, smiling at him. "Are you telling me you have made enemies over the years?"

He smiled and laughed. "Maybe a few. But they tend to be locked up or a long ways from a place like this."

They chatted for a few moments, then Sarge got a serious look on his handsome face. "I had an idea after I woke up."

"On the case of something else?"

"Case," he said.

She nodded. "Want to wait for Robin?"

He shook his head and looked slightly worried. "I would rather run it past you first and have you shoot it down than both of you laugh at me at this point. Fragile male ego and all that."

She laughed and indicated that he go ahead. She had no doubt his ego was far from fragile, but it made her feel great that he was already trusting her enough to talk with her about things he might not mention in front of others.

"I have an idea where the cars might be going," Sarge said. "I think they are going into the tunnels."

It took her a moment to realize just what he was talking about. Then it dawned on her and she nodded and sat back, thinking. Around them the sounds of laughter and conversations seemed to fade slightly.

When Las Vegas first started growing, flash floods tended to wipe out areas of it regularly, including roads and some buildings, so the city in conjunction with the county, built a vast network of concrete storm drains, called "the tunnels" by locals under the desert to take the run-off.

The tunnels were like a vast spider web under Las Vegas and for decades and decades they just were added on to seemingly without much pattern or thought as Las Vegas expanded.

The tunnels varied from around thirty feet across and ten feet tall to the size of mine shafts four feet wide and eight feet tall. All had concrete on all four sides. She had been down into the tunnels near the entrances a few times on murder scenes, but had had no desire to go farther into the pitch darkness of the hundreds and hundreds of miles of concrete.

Now the tunnels were known as shelter for the homeless from both the heat and the cold. No one knew how many, but the estimates ranged from five hundred people to far higher in numbers.

Full families lived down there in makeshift houses, often up on wooden pallets to get above the small amounts of water that sometimes ran through the concrete tunnels.

Pickett figured the tunnels were at least better than being on the streets or in a car in the wind and cold and hot sun of the seasons.

But not much.

She looked up at Sarge, who seemed to be thinking a long ways away from their table at the moment.

"Did you check to see if the tunnels ran under or near that August Tux Shop area?"

He came back into his eyes and nodded. "That area of the tunnels is so deep and so far away from most of the tunnel entrances, very few people have been in there, at least that I could find reference to before dinner."

"Wouldn't city and county maintenance people check the tunnels regularly?" Pickett asked.

"I'm sure they do every year or so, but if something was dug off to one side of the tunnels and then hidden, they would never see it," he said.

"You think they might be driving the cars out?" Pickett asked.

She doubted they were, considering that all the large tunnel entrances were heavily monitored. Cars coming out of the tunnels without going in would surely be noticed eventually.

Sarge shook his head. "I don't think so. I'm betting they are all still down there somewhere. It would take nothing to dig hidden rooms off to the sides of some of the deep tunnels in that area, let the water slowly take out the sand and dirt on the occasional storm."

"Wow," she said, laughing and shaking her head. "That must have been a hell of a nap."

He smiled. "I've always said I do my best thinking while asleep."

She laughed and at that moment Robin walked up and sat down. "Do I get to hear the joke?"

"Not a joke," Pickett said, looking intently at her partner. "Sarge may have figured out where all the cars have been going."

Robin stopped and stared at Pickett, her cloth napkin halfway unfolded.

"The tunnels," Pickett said. "They've been hiding them all off the tunnels."

All Robin could do was just blink, the perfect response.

# CHAPTER TWENTY-FOUR

*October 19th, 2016*
*Las Vegas, Nevada*

Sarge couldn't remember a fancy dinner that he had enjoyed as much as this one. Even his crazy idea about the cars being in the storm drains hadn't ruined it.

And Pickett looked fantastic in a light blue jacket, a white blouse and pearl earrings that seemed to set off her beautiful brown hair and wide smile. He was really glad he had decided to put on a jacket as well. He would have felt really out of place beside her. She just looked wonderful and he had no memory of being this attracted to a woman in a very long time.

They had talked about the case, about their lives, about Will's business, about Sarge's time as a security guard after he first retired, and so much more. And, of course, they had all talked glowingly about their kids. After all, that's what parents their age did.

And from the sounds of it, they all had fantastic kids. Clearly they had all been lucky, especially raising kids while being a detective. Nothing ever easy about that.

As they all three declined the dessert menu and went for coffee instead, Robin brought the case back up again.

"We're getting even more reports in various places about the missing being seen in voyeur videos. Mostly just living in some house somewhere that is filmed twenty-four-seven in every room."

Sarge sat back with that. He just couldn't wrap his mind around why someone, or some group, would do this to so many people. But with the vast amount of money to be made from porn, maybe that was the core of everything here, from the wedding rapes to men and women being taken.

Stranger things had happened over his years as a detective, but not at this scale they were facing here.

"Any way to trace any of the film stuff?"

"No chance," Robin said, shaking her head. "And the money into the August Tux Shop family seems to be a bust as well at the moment, but we are still digging very, very carefully."

"You want me to get Mike and his people looking deeper?" Sarge asked.

Robin shook her head. "At the moment we're all right. But we might need that at some point. Will and his people just won't cross a few lines, but they have no problem letting others cross those lines for them."

Sarge nodded. He was clearly going to enjoy meeting Will at some point.

"So how about after the coffee we walk over to my place," Pickett said, "and get on a big screen computer and see if we can make sense of the old maps of the tunnels."

Robin nodded and reached for her phone. "I'll have Will e-mail you all the links and data about the tunnels in that August

Tux Shop area, including how big they are and how often they are checked."

Sarge liked the idea and liked how they were both taking his tunnel idea seriously. And the more he thought about it, the more he liked the idea as well. It was crazy enough to make sense.

"Can you get him to send the information as to how far underground those car sensing devices would work?" Pickett asked.

Sarge nodded to that as well.

Then, for the next fifteen minutes, the three sipped their coffee, maybe the best-tasting coffee Sarge could remember, and talked about cats. And how Pickett was going to help him find a cat or two when this was all over. And how Robin thought it was about time Pickett got another cat or two as well.

Sarge liked that conversation because it meant that Pickett planned on spending time with him even after they stopped working on this case. And he liked that more than he wanted to think about.

# CHAPTER TWENTY-FIVE

*October 19th, 2016*
*Las Vegas, Nevada*

Pickett felt instantly worried as she and Robin and Sarge got off the elevator at the top of the Ogden and moved to her door. There were only two other doors off this lobby and she had never met any of the other residents of the other two condos. She didn't even know who they were and had never bothered to ask. They seemed to be very quiet people.

She now just hoped her place was clean and she hadn't left underwear or something draped over a chair. She couldn't remember the last time anyone had been in her condo. More than likely it was right after she moved in when she made dinner for Robin and Will.

Luckily, she hired a cleaning service every week to take off the rough edges. Even retired, she hated cleaning things. She seemed to always think of better things to do.

As she unlocked her door and led them into the tiled

entranceway, she felt as if she was seeing the place through Sarge's eyes. Her brown wood floors, tan and brown soft cloth furniture, and dark oak bookcases filled to overflowing gave the place a comfortable and lived-in feel.

She made herself take a deep breath and headed for the kitchen after slipping out of her shoes She never wore shoes around her apartment. Shoes were for going out.

"Coffee, water, or Diet Coke is all I got at the moment."

"Water," Robin said.

"Same," Sarge said. "And wow is this a nice place. Comfortable."

He had moved to the big windows looking along the Strip. The view was spectacular and one of the reasons Pickett had bought the place. But it pleased her that Sarge thought it comfortable as well.

"Thanks," she said, pulling out three bottles of water from her fridge.

"Where are you hiding the computer?" Robin said as Pickett handed her a bottle.

"Office through that door there," Pickett said, pointing to a closed door beside the kitchen. She wasn't sure why she always kept that door closed, but she did. Sort of like an unofficial boundary between work and the comfort of her home.

"How big is this place?" Sarge asked as she handed him a bottle and then they turned to follow Robin into the office.

"Three bedroom, two bath, about twenty-six hundred square feet," Pickett said as Robin dropped into Pickett's black leather office chair and got the big Mac computer started up.

"Wow!" Sarge said.

"You ought to see the deck," Pickett said, smiling at him. "I spend a lot of evenings and early mornings out on that deck just staring out over this stupid city I love so much."

"With a view like this," he said, pointing at the big windows behind them, "it would be a crime to not stare at it."

Robin took only a moment to get the map of the storm tunnels under Vegas opened. She did a few quick strokes and a circle appeared in one area off the strip.

"Where the cars vanish from tracking," she said, pointing at the circle.

Pickett was surprised at how large that area actually was and she and Sarge stood behind Robin in front of the computer.

"Only two tunnels run under this area," Robin said. "One is a really old one and it's down about a hundred feet and the second is a newer one from thirty years ago. Both are too far for any kind of ground penetrating radar."

"Can you isolate just those two tunnels on the map and show the entrances on either end?" Sarge asked.

Robin nodded and a moment later it was clear that the older tunnel merged into the newer tunnel on both ends. And it was smaller.

"Any bet that old tunnel is blocked off on both ends, with only small holes to allow the water to run out," Sarge said.

"No bet," Pickett said.

She just kept staring at the screen. Could it really be possible that the old tunnel running close to the August Tux Shop was where all those people had disappeared into?

And if so, why?

And could any of them still be alive down there? That idea just made her stomach tighten into a knot.

This entire thing was a nightmare.

# CHAPTER TWENTY-SIX

*October 19th, 2016*
*Las Vegas, Nevada*

Sarge had known from the first night that Pickett lived in the Ogden, but he had never expected her to be his neighbor.

On the penthouse floor.

Her view faced the Strip, but he was pretty sure she didn't know that his penthouse next door was two stories tall and had an almost three-hundred-and-sixty-degree view of the entire area on the upper level.

He couldn't believe that in the years they had both lived here they had never run into each other in an elevator or either of the lobbies or in the parking garage. He was sure he would have recognized her and remembered if he had.

And he was a little worried about what she was going to think when she discovered he lived next door. His living in the Ogden had just never come up in conversation over the last two days. He wasn't sure how he would feel considering his interest in her. He had a hunch he would like that she was close, but he was going to have to tell her soon or there would be other problems.

But there was no doubt that as ex-cops, they both lived pretty darned good. He loved how she had decorated her place. His looked similar, with brown tones and lots of books. And he loved how she got comfortable in front of them when she came in.

For about fifteen minutes Robin explored every angle about the tunnels they could think of. He liked standing next to Pickett watching Robin work on details from the tunnels. It felt right to be beside Pickett.

The old tunnel had been dug out of solid sandstone and was about ten paces wide and eight feet high. And it hadn't been inspected since the city had closed it up in 1996.

Finally, there was no more to get from the computer so they all headed back out into the living room and sat down.

Robin sat in a large brown chair facing a large brown and tan cloth couch. Pickett sat on the couch near one end, clearly her favorite spot and Sarge sat on the other end. A large coffee table filled the space between the chair and the couch. It was covered with a few books, one without a dust jacket that was clearly in the process of being read. Sarge couldn't see the title, but he was very curious.

"So what next?" Pickett asked.

"We keep digging," Robin said. "I would like to know what we might be running into down in those tunnels before we ever go down there or send anyone else down there."

Sarge could only nod to that. "We are working on just guesses at this point anyway."

"Let's tick off what we do know," Pickett said. "We know

first off that a lot of people about to get married have gone missing over the last number of years."

Sarge again nodded, as did Robin.

"We know," Pickett said, "that their cars vanish into an area and never come out again, at least in any fashion that has been traced."

"Center of the area is the August Tux Shop," Robin said. "Which is the tie to the weddings."

"Circumstantial," Sarge said, "but the only central tie to all of the men and women disappearing that we have at the moment."

Pickett and Robin both nodded.

"And we have unsubstantiated reports that some of the vanished people have been seen in voyeur porn videos," Pickett said.

"But we have no way to check that or any money trail yet," Robin said.

"And we know for a fact that someone has hacked the marriage license records in the county," Pickett said.

Sarge had to admit they didn't have anything that pointed to anyone at all except in very general terms. They really needed to find some sort of hard evidence or this was all going to grind to a dead halt again, as all these cases had done before.

They sat in silence for a moment, then Pickett said, "Something Mac said when we talked to him is haunting me."

Sarge watched her and Robin turned to face her as well.

"Mac said this has something to do with marriage," Pickett said. "He thinks that's one of the keys."

Sarge sat back, shaking his head. "Mac was right. It does have to do with marriages. Every detail of it, actually. But not in a standard way."

"Not in a church, happily-ever-after way?" Robin asked.

Sarge shook his head. "Not at all. Weddings in this city are a major attraction to draw all types from all over the country. Right?"

Both other detectives nodded, so Sarge smiled and went on.

"Porn is a major industry as well, including wedding night porn and voyeur porn, right?"

Again both nodded.

"So our creeps set up a way to get prospective, good-looking clients to come to them, to this city. That would be the August Tux Shop and the other wedding stores they own."

"And they know their clients are coming," Robin said, "from the hacks in the marriage license data base, so they have each person's personal information before they walk through the doors."

"So you are saying that this does have to do with marriage," Pickett said, "but just as a way to find porn actors to work for free."

"Exactly," Sarge said. He knew in his gut he was right on this. For the first time some of this was making a sick sort of sense.

"So this is a sex trade problem," Robin said. "But I'm betting not a one of these victims have ever left this country."

"You think they are in the tunnels?" Pickett asked.

"I would bet most anything on it," Sarge said. "The ones that are still alive."

"So now what do we do?" Robin asked. "Not a bit of this is strong enough to get a warrant."

"You and Will and your people keep digging," Pickett said. "Carefully."

Then Pickett turned to Sarge and smiled. "We're the field team. You up for getting some help and putting together an experienced expedition into those storm drains to see what we can see? Maybe interview some homeless people down there for what they have seen?"

"I hate the idea," Sarge said. And he did. Completely. But he also knew that Pickett was right.

He smiled at her. "But I don't think we have a choice at this point. We have to find out if this crazy idea is right or not."

"For the record," Robin said, "I hate this idea as well. But I also see no choice."

"I'll call Mike Dans tomorrow morning," Sarge said. "See if we can hire him and his team to help us."

"With him along," Robin said, "I hate the idea a little less."

"Speak for yourself," Pickett said, smiling at her partner.

Sarge just laughed. And considering the stupidity of the idea they were discussing, that felt good.

"Now I could use a drink," Robin said.

"I've got what some people say is a really good white wine at my place," Sarge said. "You two up for a glass of wine before we call it a night?"

"How far do you live from here?" Robin asked.

Pickett was looking puzzled as well.

"Not far," Sarge said smiling. He pointed to Pickett's bare feet. "In fact, you won't even have to put your shoes back on."

# CHAPTER TWENTY-SEVEN

*October 19th, 2016*
*Las Vegas, Nevada*

Pickett was stunned as Sarge led them out her front door, made sure she had her key, then instead of going to the elevator, turned to the left and put a key into the door right next to hers.

"We're neighbors?" she asked, feeling completely stunned. He had said he was rich, but she had no idea he was as rich as she was.

Maybe richer.

"I didn't know either until tonight," he said. "You said you had a condo here, but I didn't expect us to both be on the same floor."

"So you two have never run into each other in the elevators or lobby or anywhere?" Robin asked.

"And never once thought to ask who my neighbors were," Sarge said.

"I didn't either," Pickett said, laughing as Sarge led them into his penthouse condo.

"Two great detectives," Robin said, shaking her head. "You might want to find out who is in that third condo on this floor just to make sure it isn't our August Tux Shop owner."

"Oh, real good plan there," Pickett said, laughing. "Wouldn't that be funny if it was him?"

Both Sarge and Robin said at the exact same time, "No."

Pickett was amazed at how comfortable she felt in Sarge's condo. In fact, it felt a lot like her place. He had decorated everything in brown tones as well, and had one full wall of oak bookcases filled completely with hardbacks on the wall that separated his place from hers. His living room windows looked to the north and east and she could imagine the beauty of the sunrises.

The ceilings over his living room were higher than hers and the windows taller, but the kitchen to the right of the main room seemed similar.

"Wow, two stories?" Robin said.

Pickett turned to see what Robin meant and saw the wide, almost grand-looking staircase leading up to a level above.

"Always wondered who had that top floor in this place," Pickett said.

"Are you really this rich?" Robin asked, staring at the place and making Sarge look slightly uncomfortable.

"Massive family inheritance the year after I quit the force," Sarge said. "Dead broke like all detectives before that. Figured a really nice place to live would be a good way to spend a little of the inheritance money and this place was open because of the recession."

"Can we see the upstairs?" Pickett asked.

Sarge smiled and said, "Be my guests."

He led the way up the staircase to a massive room at the top that had most of a complete view of all of Las Vegas and the valley and mountains around the city. His view was the same as hers, and with everything else around the valley included as well, seen clearly through the tall windows.

To Pickett it felt as if they had stepped up on the roof of the building, only the roof was covered and enclosed and had soft couches and furniture filling a central area. There were no other rooms blocking the view in any direction, so clearly all the bathrooms and bedrooms were on the main level below.

It was clear that Sarge spent a lot of time up here, judging by the pile of books and papers on the large coffee table in the middle of the room.

"Wow," Robin said moving to the middle of the room and slowly turning to take in everything. "Just wow."

Pickett glanced at Sarge. "This is just amazing."

"Sold me on the place when I saw it," he said. "And even in the summer in the day, the windows have a special tint that blocks the sun for the most part and the air conditioning can keep up with the rest. And on nice evenings such as this one, I can sit out on the deck.

He went to the side facing the Strip and slid open a wide glass door and stepped outside.

The cool night air felt wonderful to Pickett as she stepped out beside him, staring at the bright lights of the massive casinos. The deck seemed to run along the entire side of the upper floor and around to the right.

"There can't be many views like this in all of Las Vegas," Robin said.

"Costs a lot," Sarge said. "Sometimes I'm actually embarrassed to spend even the condo fees and utilities each month, considering they are more than my entire mortgage payment used to be on my old home."

"But we can't take it with us, can we?" Pickett said, laughing.

"Exactly," Sarge said, smiling. "I got my daughter set up so that if something happens to me, she is even richer than I ended up. So nothing else to do but spend some of this on a wonderful place to live. And a lot of good meals."

"Well," Robin said, "if you two don't mind, I'm going to head for home and talk with Will about maybe moving to a place with a view. Maybe that third condo up here will come open."

Pickett laughed. "You can't fool me, partner. You're going home to work and see how the research is going."

Robin smiled as she headed down the stairs. "Well, that too."

# CHAPTER TWENTY-EIGHT

*October 19th, 2016*
*Las Vegas, Nevada*

Sarge wasn't sure what to do next, considering that he was now alone with a beautiful woman in his place, something that had never happened before. It made him feel young and completely stupid, something he remembered feeling all the time when he actually had been young.

They both stared at the view from the balcony for a moment, then Sarge asked the question he needed to ask first. "Does it bother you that I am your neighbor?"

Pickett laughed and shook her head, looking up at him. "Not in the slightest. I kind of like it, to be honest. Does it bother you I live right down there?"

She pointed down at her deck under his.

He laughed, realizing that he liked having her that close. "Not in the slightest either. So how about that glass of wine I offered. Clearly Robin wasn't into drinking."

"She's married," Pickett said, smiling. "She's forgotten how to have a good time."

"And we've remembered?" Sarge asked.

"Planning to remember," Pickett said. "And yes, I would love that glass of wine."

He liked the sounds of that a lot and all worry about them being neighbors just vanished. In fact, it looked like it might be a real advantage.

"You want to wait here or take a peek into my wine cellar?" Sarge asked.

"You have another level to this place?"

"Well," Sarge said, "from here we do have to go downstairs to get to the wine."

"This I've got to see," Pickett said, laughing.

Sarge let her lead off the patio and he slid the door closed and then followed her down the stairs as she just kept staring around.

"This place is amazingly comfortable," she said when she reached the bottom of the stairs, staring first at the kitchen, then around at the living room.

He loved to hear her say that. Pleased him more than he wanted to admit and again he realized he was back being a kid, worried about how a girl would think of something he did.

At his age, that actually felt nice, not at all like the panic he had felt when young.

"So is your place," he said. "I was surprised how similar our tastes were and I love that you had a lot of books scattered around."

"I liked the same thing about your place," she said.

He turned and led her down a wide hallway going away from the kitchen and toward the bedrooms. He had had the bookshelves along the wall of the hallway custom built just for fun. They were full completely of books he had read and others he planned on reading at some point.

About halfway down the hallway he stopped and made sure she was watching, then pulled out a book from the second shelf from the top. There was a click and the wall moved inward revealing an oak table and beyond the table a glass wall showing a large room of wine on racks beyond.

This had been a fourth bedroom when he bought the place, but it had just sat empty before he remodeled.

"You've got to be kidding me," she said, laughing and clapping her hands.

Her laugh sounded like a kid in a candy store and that just made him smile more than he already was smiling.

"Always wanted a secret room behind a bookcase," he said, feeling very proud of his wine room as they stepped inside. "I needed to build a climate-controlled room for a decent wine collection anyway, so why not go all the way. Having too much money can create things like this."

She laughed. "I flat love it."

"There's more," he said.

He turned and pushed a button and another wall to the right of the door slid back revealing a major computer terminal and half-dozen large screens.

He had a bunch of the research he had done on the desk beside the terminal and some printouts of the area and a large printout of the tunnels.

"This functions as a security system for the condo as well as a major computer set-up for research," he said. "Mike Dans' people set this up for me when I first moved in here."

"Wow, just wow," she said.

She looked up at him, staring with those wonderful brown

eyes of hers at him. Then she said, "Thank you for showing me this. Makes me feel like a kid again."

"Thanks for letting me show it to you," he said. "I feel the same way."

With that, he turned and opened up the glass door into the climate-controlled part of the room and picked a special white wine, something he had been saving for a special moment.

This sure seemed like a special moment to him.

Very special.

# CHAPTER TWENTY-NINE

*October 19th, 2016*
*Las Vegas, Nevada*

Pickett did as Sarge instructed and went into the living room near the kitchen while he opened the wine. She sat down on the couch facing the windows. She couldn't believe how comfortable she felt with him and how wonderful his place was.

She felt just as comfortable here as she did in her own condo. And being right next door was a wonderful benefit no matter what they decided to do with a relationship. She had a hunch that Sarge could be a very, very close friend.

And she had to admit, she was hoping for more than friendship. A lot more, but she had to remind herself that she had only known Sarge for less than two days. It felt now like she had known him her entire life.

Strange, very strange, but it didn't scare her in the slightest. In fact, she was going to enjoy the feeling. And it seemed like he was as well.

He had been like a young boy showing her his nifty hidden room. She had loved that look on his face of pride and happiness that she had liked it as well.

And she hadn't been making it up that she had liked the room and the computer set-up. She in fact loved it.

And she really loved that upper floor with the most amazing view of all the lights of the Las Vegas valley. On a clear fall night like tonight, that had just been stunning.

He came out of the kitchen and handed her a tall crystal wine glass.

"Can I ask what you are thinking?"

She smiled at him as he sat down beside her and put his feet up on the coffee table, clearly completely relaxed with her. She liked that more than she wanted to admit to herself.

"Honestly," she said, "thinking about how much I love your place and your nifty upstairs and even wilder secret room."

He smiled. "Thank you. That means a lot to me. You are the first person I have shown it to."

She frowned and turned to him. "Not even your daughter?"

He shrugged. "Nope. She and her husband don't drink and they stay in hotels when in town for more privacy, so the only time they are here is when they allow me to cook for them. Never occurred to me that they would even appreciate it."

"Thank you," she said, holding up her wine glass to toast him. "For sharing with me."

He clinked his glass lightly against hers and then she took a sip, startled at how wonderful the wine was.

"Wow, this is something," she said.

"It is, isn't it?" Sarge said, taking a second sip and smiling. "Lott suggested I try it, so I bought a bottle for a special occasion. I think I might need to buy a few more bottles, don't you?"

"Without a doubt," she said, taking another sip of the wonderful smooth wine.

She couldn't believe how pleased she was that he thought this was a special occasion. It felt that way to her, since this was the first time in memory that she had been in a man's apartment, alone. A man she was interested in as well.

"So what are you thinking?" she asked after a moment.

"Honestly wondering where this is headed with us," he said.

She was surprised that he had been so direct, but not really. In the short time she had known him, that clearly was his way of dealing with things. Direct, honest, and straightforward.

She set her glass down on the coffee table, then took his glass from his hands and set it beside hers.

Then she turned to face him and look into his slightly worried eyes.

"I think it should go this way," she said.

She leaned up and kissed him.

It took him a moment to kiss her back, then he did, wrapping his wonderful arms around her and pulling her up close.

She was lost in the kiss. Better than any kiss she had ever remembered.

Better than her first kisses in high school.

After a moment he broke the kiss and leaned back and looked into her eyes.

He was smiling, more than likely as hard as she was.

"That was really wonderful," he said, his voice slightly husky.

"I agree, detective," she said. "But I think we need more research on this topic, don't you."

He laughed and nodded and this time he kissed her, pulling her up and against him.

And it felt heavenly to be against him.
And right.
Perfectly right.

# UNDER LAS VEGAS

# CHAPTER THIRTY

*October 20th, 2016*
*Las Vegas, Nevada*

Sarge couldn't believe that the evening had ended up in his large bed and the morning had started off with the two of them taking a shower together and soaping each other's backs.

He felt young again and seeing Pickett's beautiful naked body under the streaming water sure helped that feeling, so much so that they ended up taking a second shower after going back to bed.

He had thought that part of his life long past, and she had said the same thing. But it had been great.

Then in one of his bathrobes, carrying her clothes, she had gone back to her place to dress and he had knocked on her door fifteen minutes later.

She came out smiling. And gave him a kiss.

That was wonderful. A beautiful woman kissing him in the morning. Didn't get better as far as he was concerned.

Then they had walked together the five blocks to the Golden Nugget for breakfast.

To Sarge it all felt completely natural and when he mentioned that to her on the walk, she had laughed and agreed. "I wouldn't mind getting used to this," she had said. "Is that too forward too fast?"

He had laughed and mentioned that after what they had done last night and then again this morning, that seemed pretty slow.

She had agreed to that.

After they both had finished off their breakfasts and read the morning paper, her on her tablet and he with the actual paper, they turned their attention back to the case.

"So are we going into the tunnels?" Pickett asked.

Sarge hated the idea, but could see no other way around it. "Call Robin and see if she has any updates that will stop such lunacy. If not, I'll call Mike."

Pickett nodded and after a moment was talking with Robin on speaker phone. There was no one at any table close enough to overhear, luckily.

Robin and her computer geeks were making progress, and it all seemed to lead to the porn industry and the tunnels. No trace of any of the cars driven by a missing person had ever been found, not even a part. So the cars were clearly just being stored and there was more than enough room down in the old tunnels to do that, or to carve out new rooms.

"We have nowhere near enough evidence to get a search warrant on any of the August Tux Shop properties," Robin said. "So we can't look for any entrance from the surface."

"So we look for the evidence from below," Sarge said, nodding. "In the public areas. I'm going to call Mike Dans and hire him and his people to go with us down there."

"I'm coming as well," Robin said.

"Nope," Pickett said. "We need you right where you are at and I'm sure Mike can set up monitoring equipment so you and Will and his people can trace our movements."

"But…" Robin started to argue but Pickett cut her off.

"Partner, you know I am right," Pickett said. "So get as much information on that old tunnel as you can while we set this up with Mike."

"All right," Robin said. "Not happy."

"Not happy to be going into a tunnel either," Pickett said, smiling and winking at Sarge.

"Call me when you are set up," Robin said and clicked off.

"She gets that way," Pickett said, smiling. "But she knows I'm right. That's what annoys her."

Sarge got on the phone to Mike Dans and told him what they had found, what their suspicions were.

"You are going to need a team to go down in there," Mike said.

"That's why I called," Sarge said, glad that Mike was ahead of him a little. "I want to hire you and your team to go with me and Detective Pickett."

"No need to pay," Mike said.

"I'm paying," Sarge said. "I have more money than I know what to do with and I want you running this operation. So I want your best team that money can buy on this."

"Afraid what we are going to find?" Mike asked.

"Deathly afraid," Sarge said. "Besides, those damn storm drains scare hell out of me."

"Yeah," me too," Mike said. "Send me all your data and what you think is actually going on and where. I'll meet you at noon at the Bellagio Café so we can go over details. We'll go in right after dark."

"Thanks, Mike," Sarge said.

He clicked off the phone and looked into the worried eyes of the woman he was falling for.

"We've got a professional team," Sarge said.

"Which takes this idea up just a notch above totally nuts," Pickett said.

Sarge could only nod at that.

And try not to think about getting lost in cold, dark, concrete tunnels.

# CHAPTER THIRTY-ONE

*October 20th, 2016*
*Las Vegas, Nevada*

Pickett flat hated the idea of going down into those storm drains. The tunnels were one of the better kept secrets of Las Vegas. Tourists never knew they existed, and the homeless used them for shelter. And as far as she knew, the homeless very seldom went very far in from the entrances.

And there were a lot of entrances all over the city. Some of the major ones were outside the main freeways, but a lot of the smaller entrances were in basements of parking garages.

Las Vegas had built two separate drainage systems, often running side-by-side underground. One system took away wastewater from homes and casinos and hotels while the second system only drained away surface water. But the second system had tunnels far larger than the normal sewers to handle the rare flash floods.

And the storm drain system got a lot less attention since it was seldom used for any storms. Even when it rained, the storm drains seldom had more than a few inches running through them.

When a large storm was headed toward Vegas back in her last years on the force, the charity organizations mounted a vast rescue operation to get the homeless out of the tunnels before the flood hit. No one knows exactly how many they didn't rescue, but those tunnels had mostly filled with that storm. If anyone had been down there, they wouldn't have stood a chance.

Now she and Sarge were going down into that storm drain system, something she had never had to do as a full detective. Seemed like being retired didn't have all the benefits it was cracked up to have.

Pickett had Robin send Mike all their data and theories and all the data on where the cars disappear and told her about the meeting at lunch.

Then after breakfast Pickett and Sarge decided they were going to need to buy some supplies, since neither of them had the clothes or supplies for what they were going to attempt later in the day. So for the first time in a very long time, she went shopping with a man.

She had to admit, she liked it and he had her laughing most of the hour it took them.

They both ended up with boots that were water repellant, heavy gloves, and powerful flashlights. They would wait to talk with Mike at lunch about what more they would need.

They dropped their new supplies back at their condos, then headed for lunch at the Bellagio, getting there about twenty minutes before Mike and settling into the same booth they had spent so much time in the day before.

Around them the casino noises were muffled by the thick

green plants and the sounds of others eating and talking in the restaurant. Even the same waitress as yesterday waited on them, greeting them like old friends.

"Starting to feel like home," Sarge had said, laughing.

"Maybe on big cases we could reserve it," Pickett said.

She hoped that in the rest of their careers they wouldn't have a case this big again.

Robin was going to join them for the planning meeting so she could coordinate everything with Will and her computer people. And she really wanted to meet Mike Dans. But she hadn't arrived yet either, so Pickett decided to ask what Sarge was thinking about the plan. She actually had managed to not give it much thought.

"Trying not to," Sarge said. "I'm hoping that Mike knows someone that is an expert on the tunnels who he can trust and help us plan how we go in."

"Afraid of being monitored?"

"That and a lot more," Sarge said, nodding. "If this operation is as large as it seems to be, they will have every possible entrance to that area of the tunnels monitored. And more than likely guards and other traps for anyone getting too near the area."

Pickett sat back, slightly stunned. The idea of a firefight in the tunnels had never crossed her mind, but it sure made sense. And then something else sent a chill down her spine.

"If those people are alive down there," she said, "or some of them, we have to go in with the element of surprise."

Sarge nodded. "That's why I want to wait for both Mike and Robin on this and just try not to think about it. They are going to know how to block security cams and watch for other traps we might run into."

Pickett just shook her head. "And I thought just going into storm sewers was scary enough."

"If this actually is a million dollar porn operation," Sarge said, "and they have kidnapped and maybe killed as many people as we think they have, the tunnels are going to be the least of our worries."

She knew he was right.

Completely right.

And she couldn't see another choice but to go right into it. They couldn't legally go in and search above ground. They had no evidence at all against anyone. So they had to go into the public areas below ground.

"I hope we are wrong about what is happening down there," Sarge said, staring off at the people around them in the restaurant going about their daily lives and vacations.

"Rather start back at square one to figure out all this?" Pickett asked.

"To be wrong on this I sure would," Sarge said, nodding.

"But you don't think we're wrong, do you?"

He shook his head.

And again, she agreed with him. All her years of being a detective told her they were right.

And that meant those tunnels were going to lead them straight into hell.

# CHAPTER THIRTY-TWO

*October 20th, 2016*
*Las Vegas, Nevada*

Mike Dans arrived about the same time as Robin and joined them.

Mike looked ex-military all the way, with a shaved head, massive shoulders, and a panther-like walk. He just radiated power and confidence and Sarge loved that.

The introductions were great. Sarge introduced Robin and Pickett and then Pickett and Mike dropped into computer and job and security service shoptalk, ignoring both Sarge and Pickett.

Sarge found it funny and was glad they didn't talk about the coming mission until after they had all ordered lunch.

And it was clear to Sarge that both Robin and Pickett liked Mike almost instantly. That was good, considering what they were going to trust him with.

"So, Mike," Sarge said after the waitress left with their

orders. "Any ideas of what we might be facing and how to do it?"

"I should have a little more idea any time now," Mike said. "I have a great friend with some pretty special ground-penetrating radar equipment taking a look in that area for us right now."

Sarge was shocked at that, as clearly was Pickett and Robin.

"GPR is only good for about sixty feet in this sandy soil," Robin said.

Mike smiled. "Regular GPR, yes. My friend has invented a way for the government to go much deeper by combining the waves off of a dozen GPRs at the same time, using a massive computer to sort out the details."

"How far down can he go?" Sarge asked.

Mike smiled. "Detail will only be empty spaces and pipes and tunnels and such, but he'll get us a pretty clear picture of that area if anything is down there."

"And the shaft going down if it's under the August Tux Shop area?" Robin asked.

"He's doing a complete search of that 25 block area at the level of those two tunnels," Mike said. "After lunch, if you don't mind, Sarge, we can go up to that secret room of yours and study the results."

"No problem," Sarge said. "So you think we can get in there without being seen?"

"Into the main tunnel down there, yes," Mike said. "And we can block any security cameras and trips they might have set up along the way."

Sarge could see that Mike wasn't saying something.

"But the problem is…" Sarge said, giving him his chance.

Mike nodded. "Getting into that closed-off tunnel. I have an expert who knows where that old tunnel connections to the new tunnel are and the concrete used to close it off."

Mike dug into a folder he had brought along and set on the booth beside him. "This is a picture of that old tunnel where it meets the new tunnel."

He slid the picture to Sarge who looked at it and could feel himself shudder. That was a nightmare.

He slid it to Pickett.

The picture showed clearly the square shape of the old tunnel, now filled with concrete. And in the very center of the fill was a small square hole on the floor that was clearly drainage for any water that got down into the old tunnel. The hole was black and it looked like some sort of slime had built up on the floor of the hole.

"How big is that hole?" Pickett asked as she passed the picture to Robin.

"I'll be able to squeeze through," Mike said. "But barely."

Robin just stared at the picture and shook her head.

"So one of the most hidden and inaccessible places in Las Vegas," Sarge said.

Mike nodded. "That old tunnel entrance there is a six mile walk from the main entrance to the newer tunnel. As far as we can tell, those holes in the ends are the only places to enter that old tunnel since all access drains were closed or diverted to the new tunnel."

"Wow," Robin said, still shaking her head.

Sarge could tell that Pickett looked like she was almost in shock as the reality of what they were thinking sank in. That picture just looked damned scary. He knew Pickett was one of the bravest people who had ever carried a badge. And he seldom backed down either, but right now he was having second thoughts as well.

"So anything closer than six miles that would still be safe?" Robin asked. "I have a hunch the main entrances to that tunnel will be monitored."

"They are," Mike said, nodding.

Sarge looked up at his friend, who was looking very serious. "My man who took that picture this morning also had equipment on him that could sense monitoring. That main tunnel is under surveillance and monitoring the entire length, all nineteen miles of it. And those old tunnel entrances both have major surveillance on them, including video. He snapped that picture while just walking past like an explorer."

Silence filled the booth. Around them the casino and dining room sounds seemed to just fade back and Sarge could almost hear his heart beating.

"We really are on to something big, aren't we?" Pickett said softly.

Mike nodded.

"Shit, just shit," Robin said.

Sarge just shook his head. He had so hoped that they were wrong about the tunnels and where all those people had gone. But there was more and more evidence pointing to the fact that they were not.

And they had nowhere near enough evidence to go in with a search warrant to the August Tux Shop and try to find the entrance. And even the ground-penetrating radar, if it showed a shaft going down, wouldn't be enough evidence to prove any crime.

Somehow they needed to get into that tunnel and find those people. Or at least their cars.

At that moment the waitress brought their lunches and all four of them put the task at hand away.

But Sarge wasn't sure he could eat that much at the moment.

Pickett reached over and put her hand on his leg, then smiled at him.

She looked worried in those wonderful brown eyes, but determined.

And with that smile he felt slightly better. And her touch made him feel even better. He smiled at her and nodded.

They were not tackling all this alone. They had the best help around them they could get.

And if the radar found more under there, they were going to need to bring in even more help.

# CHAPTER THIRTY-THREE

*October 20th, 2016*
*Las Vegas, Nevada*

After lunch they headed in three cars back to the Ogden and up to Sarge's apartment. Pickett hoped that they hadn't left any sort of evidence of their wonderful night draped over a chair or something silly like that. This morning she just hadn't cared and she doubted Sarge had as well.

But now with Robin and Mike with them, Pickett felt there was no point in being embarrassed. And then she realized how silly that thought was. She was a retired grown woman. She had a hunch Robin knew exactly what had happened last night. And that was fine.

So when they got to Sarge's condo, they all headed to his secret wine room with the incredible computer set-up.

Mike took the computer chair while the three of them stood behind him. The large screens were big enough and placed high enough that there was no problem seeing what he was doing.

Mike quickly, with his fingers moving faster than Pickett could imagine typing, brought up some sort of files.

"I've got all the preliminary scans," Mike said. "Here we go. First I'm going to run this like we are looking down through the ground from a plane flying overhead."

That made sense to Pickett until the image showed up.

"This is down to one hundred and twenty feet," Mike said, pointing to an indicator on the screen.

Pickett couldn't make sense out of what she was seeing. It seemed more like a bunch of blurry lines than anything.

"Oh, shit," Mike said softly, more to himself than anyone.

"You're going to have to help me read this," Sarge said.

"Me too," Pickett said. She glanced at Robin who seemed to have seen a ghost her face was so white.

"There are fifteen or twenty city blocks of tunnels and rooms down there," Mike said.

"City blocks?" Sarge asked.

Pickett just couldn't grasp what Mike had just said.

"City blocks," Mike said, clearly not happy with what he was seeing. "It's like a rat's nest of tunnels and rooms."

Mike ran his finger on the screen, showing lines of open spaces. Pickett could see what he was outlining and it still didn't make sense.

"From the looks of this," Mike said, "There is an open area in the center of all this, with what looks to be a dozen tunnels leading to complexes of rooms off the center area."

"Those are larger than rooms," Robin said, leaning forward and indicating some other things on the big screen. Clearly she could read this kind of image from ground penetrating radar. "Those are the size of two- and three- and four-bedroom homes dug out of the dirt. Looks like tunnels lead from the main room to them."

"And they go a long ways back," Mike said.

Pickett just wanted to be sick. The people kidnapped were being held in concrete rooms right under Las Vegas. Or at least some of them. How was this even possible?

"How big is the complex?" Sarge asked, his voice low and clearly shaken. "Can you tell?"

"Going to take some time to analyze all of these images," Mike said. "But at a glance, it's huge. Maybe upward of five or six thousand rooms carved from the ground. And all are square."

Robin pointed to the screen tracing her finger along a line. "Looks to me that the pattern is a complex of five rooms that has one door off a main tunnel leading into it, like a front door of a house."

Mike was nodding. "No other way out. Each suite could hold six people easily."

"This is insane," Pickett said.

Mike nodded and changed out the images. "This is a cut through the old storm tunnel," he said. "Looks like all the new rooms down there are about the same height as the old tunnel, all leading off to the west from the tunnel."

They all kept silent as Mike went through more images, explaining what they showed. They all confirmed that there was a massive complex down there.

Massive.

Picket wished she hadn't eaten lunch now. This was far, far larger than they could handle. But she doubted these images would be enough to stop all this either.

Finally, Mike got to an image and suddenly sat back.

"Oh, God," Robin said, shaking her head. "Can you switch that area to an eagle-eye view?"

Mike nodded and switched the view. A giant mass showed up on the screen.

It took a moment before Pickett's eye saw what they were looking at.

Thousands of cars.

A hundred feet underground.

"Where does the elevator leading down to that come to the surface?" Sarge asked a moment before Pickett could.

"In the back garage of the August Tux Shop," Mike said, turning and smiling at the three detectives.

"Now we have enough for a warrant," Robin said.

"But how do we keep those people in those rooms, if they are there, from being hurt if we raid on the top floor?" Pickett asked. "There has to be some major forms of communications with that area down there back to the surface somewhere."

"Especially if they are loading out porn videos," Sarge said. "All the wedding rapes, all the voyeur videos and who knows what other things they are doing to those people. All have to be taken out of there somehow and loaded onto the dark web. Am I correct?"

Mike and Robin both nodded.

"He's right," Robin said. "We need to find that connection and control it first. I'll get Will and all our people on this."

She turned with the phone to her ear and moved out into the hallway.

Mike nodded and glanced at Sarge. "Can I use this computer? I'll get my people on this as well. You two need to talk with someone you can trust completely on this to get a warrant when we need it. We still go in tonight."

Pickett glanced at Sarge who was nodding.

"Thanks, Mike," Sarge said.

Then he and Pickett went out into the hallway and turned toward the kitchen. Pickett needed a glass of water, something to take the dry, desert feel out of her mouth.

Something to help her grasp the size of the evil they had just found.

# CHAPTER THIRTY-FOUR

*October 20th, 2016*
*Las Vegas, Nevada*

Sarge felt as if his entire body was in shock. He remembered the feeling from a few different times over the years. Always after finding something so horrid that it was impossible to believe a human being could do such a thing.

But humans could. There was no way to ever overestimate the ability of humans to commit pure evil.

"Do you think most of the missing are still alive down there?" Pickett asked as they got bottles of water in the kitchen and stood facing each other across the island. Outside the sun was bright and the sky clear, adding an even stranger feeling to the bright kitchen considering what they had learned.

"I think the ones that didn't give up on hope of rescue are alive," Sarge said.

"So more than likely there are a lot of graves down there as well," Pickett said, her voice soft.

Sarge only nodded to that. He was sure she was right.

A lot of graves.

"We are dealing with mass murderers as well as kidnapping on a scale not seen in modern America," Sarge said. His mind felt numb; he felt numb.

How was any of this even possible?

"We're still missing a lot of things, aren't we?" Pickett asked after a few long moments of both of them just standing there lost in their own thoughts.

Sarge looked at the beautiful woman he was quickly falling for and his mind came back to the task at hand like a cloud vanishing letting the sun shine through again.

"You're right, we are," he said, nodding. "Sewer, water, power, ventilation, and a ton more. All has to be provided for and hidden. And on that scale, that can't be easy. And to say nothing of the amount of food needed and waste generated."

"How many people are involved here?" Pickett asked. "An operation of this scale can't just be a few people."

Sarge grabbed his notebook and jotted down all the questions he and Pickett had just come up with.

She was right, this had to be a fairly large operation, which meant people were being paid somehow. From the people who did the kidnapping to the tech people who cleaned up and loaded out the videos to the people who ran the supplies, not even counting the security forces.

"Who can we trust?" Pickett asked, staring at him with those deep brown eyes.

"Mike's people," Sarge said. "Robin and Will's people. Julia and Lott and Andor and Doc Hill and his people. That's a lot of highly trained help there."

Pickett nodded.

At that moment Robin joined them and dug out a bottle of

water from the fridge and took a drink. "Will is as angry as I have ever seen him," Robin said. "I'm so disgusted at what we found, I am shaking."

Pickett just nodded and gave Robin a moment to take a drink and take a deep breath.

"Does Will know a judge he can trust to get the warrant on this?" Sarge asked.

Robin nodded. "My worry is the connection between the crew on the surface and the ones underground. The entire place could be rigged to explode and just kill and bury everyone."

"Shit," Sarge said. He hadn't even thought of that, but the type of people who could do this would think nothing of just burying all those people and trying to get away.

"So how do we make sure that can't happen?" Pickett asked.

Robin only shook her head and took another drink of water.

"Power," Sarge said, looking at both women. "Between lights, air, and everything else, that place has to be using the same amount of power as a decent-sized hotel. We need to find how that is being fed into the place and cut the power."

"Damn, you're right," Robin said, her phone appearing at her ear almost instantly. "Tell Mike."

Robin turned to the living room while Sarge followed Pickett back toward his computer room.

It took them only a moment to explain their fear to Mike and he nodded and turned back to the screen, talking to someone through the computer. "Find the power source."

Mike's people found it just before Robin's people did. A small two-hundred room hotel just two blocks from the August Tux Shop was drawing about three times the power it would actually need. Normally that would never be noticed. But the hotel was owned by a corporation owned by the LaPine family.

They also owned two small restaurants nearby under different corporation names.

"I'm betting those two restaurants order far more food than they sell to regular customers," Pickett said.

"So we cut the power," Sarge said. "Any thoughts on what we do next?"

"We get the warrant to hit all the above-ground locations and arrest the bastards there," Mike said, "including the owners of all this right out of their beds."

"Will and his people are on that," Pickett said. "They can make sure that will happen and have people they will vet and trust on the legal side."

"The rest of us go in the tunnels and try to get those people out of there that way," Mike said, still working the computer.

Sarge glanced at Pickett who looked pale, but was nodding.

Sarge didn't like the idea, but they had no choice at this point. And Mike and his trained men and women would be leading the way in.

Sarge nodded to Pickett. They could do this.

All that mattered now was getting all those people out of there and safe. If there really were people still alive down there.

# CHAPTER THIRTY-FIVE

*October 20th, 2016*
*Las Vegas, Nevada*

Pickett felt so at home in Sarge's place that when she ordered pizza for them, she first gave her condo address. Sarge corrected her with a smile. She really, really wanted this to be all over so that she and Sarge could just relax a little, as retired persons were supposed to do, and get to know each other even better.

Both of them had been spending the entire afternoon working over the plan for the evening rescue, trying to make sure that no detail was missed.

They had gone over and over all the tunnel diagrams and the ground penetrating radar images of the complex.

Pickett thought she could almost walk some of it in the dark which she might have to and that scared her more than the idea of a possible gun battle.

The plan, on the surface, seemed simple, which also bothered her.

Mike and his people were going to cut the power to the entire place and hope that there was no real backup power below. Or at least not enough backup power that would allow them to blow up the entire place. That was a risk they were going to have to take.

Then Mike and his people would, at the same time as the power went down, block all surveillance in the entire area, both above ground and below.

Then Mike's people inside the new tunnel would open up the entrances to the old tunnel. And then they would go in and take care of what resistance there was in guards.

Mike said he didn't expect much, but they were going in strong from both ends to make sure no one got away.

Robin said that she and Will agreed. They didn't think there would be many guards at all underground, since with the layout of the complex and everything being recorded at all times, there was no real need.

Robin just wished they could find the feeds to those rooms being sent out, but so far no luck on that.

At the same time, Will's people with police they could trust would be taking care of the arrests on the surface, including the entire LaPine family that owned the August Tux Shop, the hotel, and the restaurants.

Pickett and Sarge and Robin's job was to get the kidnapped victims out while Mike's people secured everything and made sure there were no traps or hidden explosives.

Pickett and Sarge and Robin had split up how they would take the large complex and what they would say to people as they went in.

Once the victims were on their way out, Will and the police would meet the victims at the mouth of the new tunnel and take them to a staging area and for medical attention.

Anyone not able to walk out on their own would be cared for by emergency techs as soon as the complete all-clear was given.

All effort was going to be made to keep the press from even getting a whiff of the fact that a lot of missing people had suddenly been found for at least a few days, until families could be notified.

At least Pickett hoped they were going to find a lot of missing people. They had no evidence but the huge cavern of cars to really back up their assumption that the missing would be down there.

But her gut said they would be right. She just hoped that a lot of the missing would be there and not in mass graves in some back cave.

The three of them had talked for almost an hour on what they would say to those being freed from the rooms. And what they might run into in a way of resistance of pure fear from the survivors. Some of those poor souls had been locked in those rooms for over eight or nine years. Being freed suddenly would not be an easy thing to grasp for them.

Pickett had no doubt about that. She couldn't imagine getting ready for the happiest day of your life, your wedding, and then suddenly being kidnapped and held in a concrete box with no windows and one locked door and no way to know where you were.

A horror story by any standards.

# DOWN INTO HELL

# CHAPTER THIRTY-SIX

*October 20th, 2016*
*Las Vegas, Nevada*

Sarge climbed out of Pickett's Jeep SUV and looked around the lower level of the concrete parking garage just one block off the strip. No cars were down this far and the place had a moldy smell.

Pickett climbed out of the driver's side and stretched and came around the car to him.

They both knew they were being monitored by the kidnappers. At the bottom level of this garage, about fifty paces from where they had parked, was a service access into the main storm drain just about a quarter mile from where the old tunnel was walled off.

They had to go down nine flights of stairs to get to it, but it was a logical way to go in.

As soon as Mike gave the word, all surveillance and all

power to both the main areas above ground and the entire complex below ground would be cut.

At that point the police and Will's people would raid all the above ground property and make arrests.

Sarge glanced around, making sure he and Pickett were alone. He knew they weren't really alone because three of Mike's men were already staged on the floor above and another was pretending to be a homeless man sleeping in one corner with a shopping cart that happened to be full of weapons and other things needed underground.

All four were former Special Forces, as were the other five coming in near the other tunnel entrance. Robin was with them.

It was seven-fifty-eight in the evening. They had two minutes.

Pickett came up to Sarge, put her arms around his neck and pulled his head down and kissed him before he even had a chance to realize what she was doing.

That surprised him and pleased him more than he wanted to admit and he went with the kiss, pressing back into her and holding her as well.

They spent one of the two minutes in the kiss until she finally released him and pushed back, smiling.

He knew he was smiling as well. He could feel it.

"For luck?" he asked.

"More of a promise for later," she said, smiling.

"Let's be careful and make damn sure there is a later," he said.

She nodded to that. "That idea I like."

"Stand ready, everyone," Mike said in both their ears through their com links. "Mission is a go. Cutting power and surveillance in twenty seconds."

Both Sarge and Pickett nodded and smiled at each other as they waited.

It felt to Sarge like a very long twenty seconds.

Then Mike said, "Everyone go."

Sarge nodded to Pickett as they both turned back to the SUV.

Pickett clicked open the back hatch and both of them put on vests and grabbed their guns and some extra ammunition. Sarge didn't expect them to need the guns with Mike's people going in ahead, but they were taking them just in case.

Both made sure their badges were in clear view as well. The vests said Las Vegas Police on both front and back. They both wore helmets with LED lamps in the front and both carried first aid and extra small LED flashlights in small packs.

They had just finished and closed the latch when the three men from the level above headed for the door now guarded by the one man who had been pretending to be homeless.

Sarge and Pickett reached the door to the tunnel entrance as the first three men went through. One of Mike's men would follow them down for protection.

All four of Mike's men were in full combat gear and their faces were streaked black. All carried assault rifles and packs on their backs.

"It's clear of scanning," one man said and started down the metal staircase moving silently and quickly.

The staircase looked like a standard garage staircase with concrete walls and concrete on the runners. There were lights spaced evenly all the way down and only a couple had burnt out. Sarge felt like he was descending into hell and if this operation went south, that might be exactly what he was doing.

They all moved surprisingly silently until they reached the

access door to the modern storm tunnel. At points, Sarge felt like he was tiptoeing to make sure he made no noise at all.

The man in the lead again checked a device on his arm, nodded, and then whispered, "Still clear."

Sarge watched as the guy opened the door and went through low and to the right while the man behind him went through low and to the left.

"Clear," the voice said softly and the third followed and Sarge and then Pickett followed, clicking on the LED lamps on their heads as they went.

All six of them had on their head lamps and had spread out.

The storm tunnel was all concrete on four sides, with water marks and debris along the center from the last floods. The ceiling was about eight feet overhead and Sarge could almost touch it. The entire thing was about as wide as a double car garage.

It smelled of damp earth and some rot and felt very claustrophobic and frightening with the shadows from their lights moving like bad dreams on the walls.

Sarge had not thought of himself as afraid of caves or tunnels, but at the moment, with the four special forces crew going up against some clearly smart and prepared enemies, being in this tunnel just flat scared him.

He glanced at Pickett as they headed off down the tunnel to the right. She seemed to be doing fine, but her eyes were large.

He had a hunch, his were as well.

# CHAPTER THIRTY-SEVEN

*October 20th, 2016*
*Las Vegas, Nevada*

Pickett couldn't remember another time in her long career that she had felt this afraid and this out of control. And being out of control scared her more than she wanted to think about.

And the tunnel and the creepy shadows their lights were casting made it worse.

Far worse.

They were a long ways from the bright lights and the excitement and people on the streets overhead. They might as well have been on another world down here.

It took them only a minute to reach the walled-up entrance to the old tunnel. As the picture they had studied showed, there was only a small hole about the size of an attic trap door at floor level. It was stained with black from the seepage of water over the decades.

The man with the scanning device moved up to the hole,

stuck the device in and then said softly, "Clear. Mike, we are in position and setting charges."

"The other team is also in position at the other entrance," Mike said through their communications link. Picket was amazed at how clear his voice was in her ear. It was as if he was standing right beside her.

Two of the men quickly set devices in a rectangle about the size of a large front door while the other two took positions guarding up and down the tunnel in both directions.

Pickett and Sarge moved over with their back against the same wall and turned off their lights, not saying anything. The two guarding the tunnel in both directions had both turned off their lights as well, so now the only light was from the two working around the hole.

Seemed like time stretched at that point and she forced herself to take long, slow, deep breaths.

After a moment Sarge touched her arm and she put a hand on his hand and squeezed. This was all scaring her to death, and considering what she had seen in all her years of being a detective, that sort of surprised her.

And clearly Sarge was nervous as well. But the plan was solid and above them the police and Mike's people were taking down everyone associated with any of the businesses.

Will and the Chief of Police had presented a judge they had cleared of any chance of connection to the August Tux Shop family with the evidence they had all compiled. The judge gave the Chief a sweeping search and arrest warrant that covered above ground and below ground and all personal homes with the words, "Get these sons-of-bitches."

Mike and Will had convinced the Chief that they didn't dare let too many detectives in on the raid since there was no telling if any of them worked for these scum. And with the help of Sarge and Pickett, they had convinced the Chief it would be better if Mike's people with help from the Cold Poker Gang members took care of the underground threats first.

At the same time as the raid, Will's computer people would download all computer information to make sure there was no chances of anything being destroyed.

Pickett wondered how all the raids were going. But her priority, the most important thing she could think about was rescuing anyone who might still be alive down here.

She took another deep breath and squeezed Sarge's hand again. Even with trained fighting forces with them, this was still the scariest thing Pickett had ever done.

"Ready," one of the two men said as they stepped back away from the devices they had planted, pressing themselves against the wall on either side of the small hole.

"Ready," the other team said just a fraction of a second later.

"Blow them," Mike's voice said.

Pickett didn't have a chance to get her hands over her ears to muffle the explosion and it ended up she didn't need to. The sound was more like someone dropping something heavy on the ground right near where she was standing.

Very little sound.

Just a very solid thud.

Sarge squeezed her hand and let go as they started toward the door-sized hole in the concrete. They both clicked on their lights as they approached the light dust cloud rolling away from the new door-sized hole in the concrete. The two men who had set the charges were already through the hole.

"Clear," one of them said after a moment.

The concrete debris in the doorway was nothing more than

powder now as Picket went through. Not even a piece left big enough to stumble over.

This older tunnel was lower and she could touch the ceiling easily. And a lot narrower and it smelled of rot and sewer and the air felt stale and heavy.

Three of Mike's people were at full run forward at this point with only one of the soldiers holding back with her and Sarge. That was the plan, for three to move in quickly the quarter mile along the old tunnel before she and Sarge and the fourth soldier came along as backup.

She had no doubt they wouldn't be needed as backup. It was to keep her and Sarge safe.

As they moved, as silently as they could, she kept expecting to hear gunshots ahead. The lights from the three had vanished around a slight bend in the tunnel.

Nothing.

They should be at the main area by now.

No gunshots.

Just the sound of her own breathing in her ears.

And the silence of a long-abandoned tunnel.

# CHAPTER THIRTY-EIGHT

*October 20th, 2016*
*Las Vegas, Nevada*

Sarge moved as quietly as he could down the tunnel. It felt claustrophobic even more than the larger tunnel they had just come from. He almost felt as if he would hit his head at times, so he walked slightly hunched over.

Ahead there was no sound at all.

He would have expected gunshots, but he knew the three men ahead would have switched over to night vision and might have just taken out anyone silently who might have been there guarding the tunnel.

From the images they had gotten, they knew that an artificial large room had been built off of one side of the old tunnel. And from there, the vast maze of rooms seemed to spread out through the ground.

The victim's cars were all off to the other side of the old tunnel in a massive room.

Beside him Pickett seemed to be doing better than he was. He had no idea that tunnels could bother him this much. Once this was done he hoped to live the rest of his life without ever going underground in a tunnel again.

Especially a tunnel that was only a few inches taller than he was and smelled of mold and busted sewer lines.

Suddenly, the word "Clear" sounded in his ear.

"Clear here as well," another said.

"Underground secured," another said. "No one was home."

Mike's voice came back in Sarge's ear loud and strong. "Well done. Wait for the detectives to arrive on scene before opening up any of the doors in the maze area. And stick with them."

"Copy that," the response came back.

Sarge glanced over at Pickett who looked intent as they picked up their pace to just under a jog.

Sarge was damned happy there was no one down here. They had all believed that might be the case. There would be no need to have anyone remain down here if all the doors were secured and there was no way for anyone to escape so far underground, especially if every inch of the place was monitored.

But they had had no choice but to go in expecting a force here.

Sarge and Pickett reached the large room that had been cut out of the tunnel just as Robin and her escort did from the other direction.

"Hold positions," Mike's voice said loudly in Sarge's ear. "We are bringing the lights back up and will be able to follow your progress on the monitors from here as you work your way into the maze area."

"That's great news," Robin said, nodding as she stood with Pickett and Sarge in the large open area. It looked like nothing more than a wide area in the tunnel and some garbage had been piled off to one side as if some homeless person was living there. One steel door blocked the way into the maze beyond.

Two of the special forces men were studying the door and then one said softly, "Mike, we have a problem here. Hold on bringing up the power."

"Copy," Mike said.

The other men in Mike's team quickly moved the three detectives back along the tunnel and out of direct sight of the door. Then the men spread out, moving silently and fading into the shadows almost like ghosts, leaving the detectives standing with their backs against the wall and alone.

Sarge had no idea what the two might have seen exactly at the big metal door, but if he had to bet, it would be explosives. The one thing they all had feared.

They stood in the tunnel for what seemed like an eternity, no one talking, until finally Mike's man said, "We have the door cleared. Let us go through and see what we find on the inside."

"Copy that," Mike said.

Sarge could hear a slight thump and then the sound of a heavy metal door opening slowly.

The sound was damn creepy in the old concrete tunnel.

Beside him Pickett actually shuddered, then laughed softly.

Then there was nothing again.

Silence.

And pure, complete silence in the small, underground concrete tunnel possibly filled with explosives was about as loud as anything Sarge had ever heard.

# CHAPTER THIRTY-NINE

*October 20th, 2016*
*Las Vegas, Nevada*

Pickett found herself almost holding her breath as the seconds of intense silence ticked on and on.

They were mostly standing in the dark and she knew the former Special Forces team were around them, but she couldn't see a one of them.

This was every nightmare she had ever had as a child and when that big metal door had opened with a scraping sound, it was everything she could do to just not bolt.

And then she had laughed at her own fear. She hoped not loud enough for anyone to hear. The laugh had helped.

After what seemed like the longest time, one of the Special Forces men said, "Mike, this entire place looks like it is rigged to explode."

Sarge looked at Pickett at the same time as she looked up at him in the dim light. She could see he was as worried as she felt, not for her own life but for all the victims they expected were in that place.

"All are set on two-hour timers and all the timers are going," the man said. "No motion detectors or any other problems. Just straight timers. No telling if we could find and disarm them all in time."

"We'll look for the security system up here to shut them down," Mike said, his voice clearly angry. "In the meantime, you work with the detectives to get anyone that is locked up down there out of there. Check each door as well for explosives."

"Copy that," the man said.

"People," Mike said, "we are switching to the backup plan and bringing everyone who can climb stairs up that nine-story stairwell into the parking garage. We'll stage medical and transportation help there. I have five more teams with detectives headed to help now in the evacuation, if there is one needed. Follow the search pattern we set up and detectives let my people clear an area before going into any space in that complex."

Pickett nodded. They had prepared for this and Mike was issuing orders clearly and calmly.

One of the former Special Forces men appeared next to Sarge and said, "Detective, you are with me. Stick close."

The guy was about as tall as he was and had huge shoulders and black on his face. Sarge knew better than to ask the man's name.

Sarge nodded and then smiled at Picket as one of Mike's men appeared in front of her and said the same thing. Her escort was as tall as Sarge and just as strong looking.

A moment later they were through the big metal door and into what looked like a modern living room with a low concrete ceiling. In the lights from their headlamps, Pickett could see couches, a small kitchen, and a number of computer stations.

Considering they were nine stories underground, it felt comfortable and looked completely normal.

A dozen large hallways led off from the one main room and Pickett followed Mike's man down the one to the far right as they had planned.

Pickett knew the hallway branched a number of times and contained over three-dozen suites of room. They had figured in this instance, if they had to evacuate anyone down here quickly, they would start with the closest suite of rooms and work to the back.

Mike's man stopped at the first large steel door and did a quick inspection as Pickett watched from a few steps away, then ran a hand-held device over the entire door, then nodded.

"It's clear, detective. But explosives all along this hallway."

He pointed up at the small devices that looked like small smoke alarms and Pickett nodded. She couldn't think about that now.

Mike's man put a small device near the latch and there was a low thud and the door pushed inward.

Mike's man stayed to one side and Pickett stayed to the other, backs pressed against the wall. Nothing exploded and no gunfire, so Mike's man went in first, low and to the right and Pickett went in low and to the left.

What they faced in their lamp-light was a replica of a modern living room, right down to couches, chairs, television, paintings on the walls. There were even fake windows with blinds drawn.

A light carpeting covered the floor.

To one side sat a large modern kitchen and a dining area that could hold six. It was tiled in a modern-looking pattern.

There was no one in sight, but even in the dim light Pickett could see all the cameras in the upper corners of the rooms.

These poor people had been recorded doing everything every moment of every day.

Pickett just shuddered. One of her worst nightmares.

Mike's man went silently down the hallway off the living room, checking for explosives before signaling the all clear.

"Suites are not rigged that I can tell," he said to Mike.

"Las Vegas Police!" Pickett shouted. "Anyone in here?"

She opened the first hallway door and was greeted by a man sitting up in bed, looking both shocked and scared. The room was large and well-furnished with a desk and computer and everything.

"Get dressed quickly," Pickett said. "We're getting you out of here. Wait for us by the kitchen."

The poor guy nodded and climbed out of bed,

Two more of the hallway doors opened and two women stuck their heads out to be met by Mike's man pointing a gun at them. Both were wearing pajamas.

"Las Vegas Police," Pickett said as Mike's man lowered his weapon. "Get on your robe, we're getting you out of here. Hurry."

There were three more in their rooms, all scared and surprised. But as far as Pickett could tell, they looked healthy.

By the time Pickett and Mike's man had them headed out of the door and into the main room and then out in to the drainage tunnel, ten minutes had passed.

Pickett knew that was far too long.

One of the men and two of the women were crying, but all looked unhurt, at least physically. Pickett didn't want to think about the mental damage this had done to them. She didn't want to know how long they had been locked up. She would find all that out later.

Sarge and Robin both had a group of six victims each as

well and all of them seemed to converge on the main living room at the same time.

Eighteen victims in ten minutes.

They had less than ninety minutes left if Mike and his people couldn't get the explosives stopped.

That wasn't enough time to even begin to get out everyone that might be down here.

Not even close.

They needed a lot more help to get here very, very quickly.

Or they needed Mike to find a way to disarm those explosives.

# COUNTING DOWN A VERY SHORT TIME

# CHAPTER FORTY

*October 20th, 2016*
*Las Vegas, Nevada*

Sarge wasn't letting himself think about the horror he had walked into. Six people, locked away in what looked like a large six-bedroom home, recorded every moment of every day.

The level of sickness here just made him want to stop, but he couldn't. They didn't have much time to rescue all the people that might be down here. Over the years this place had taken thousands. No telling how many still survived.

When he and Mike's man left the first group of rescues in the drainage tunnel and turned back into the main living room area, he said clearly, "Mike, we are going to need a lot more help."

"Seven teams are on the way now and will arrive in less than ten minutes, another ten teams will be on site in twenty with more following," Mike said. "And Will and I are working to find the connection to the explosives and try to shut it off when everyone is clear or our time is about to run out."

"Thank you," Sarge said, as he and the former Special Forces man assigned to him ran back down the hallway toward the next door to the next suite. Mike's man checked the door much quicker this time and blew it open and they didn't hesitate, but went in low and quick.

Again, as the first one they had gone into, the suite was a massive living room, with a kitchen off to one side and a dining room. It looked normal, like any home.

Disturbingly normal.

"Las Vegas Police," he shouted as they started down the hall.

A man looking angry opened one bedroom door right ahead of them. "What are you doing here?"

The guy had a gun at his side. Clearly he was one of the jailers spending a night with one of the victims.

"Drop the gun," Sarge said.

The guy just sneered and raised the gun.

Both Sarge and Mike's man fired, twice each.

The guy went down like the sack of shit he was, a shocked look on his face.

"We have some jailers in the apartments," Mike's man said into the general com link. "Go cautiously. One is down and won't be breathing anytime soon, but no telling how many more of these creeps are down here."

"Copy that," Mike said. "Be alert, people. Don't get sloppy and in too much of a hurry."

Sarge stepped over the pile of garbage they had just shot as the other bedroom doors opened and more victims looked out.

Sarge knew he had to be in a hurry, otherwise a lot of people were going to die.

And they had no idea how many.

One more thing he didn't want to think about at the moment.

# CHAPTER FORTY-ONE

*October 20th, 2016*
*Las Vegas, Nevada*

Pickett heard the shots like a distant pop echoing through the corridors. She was relieved when she heard that Sarge and one of Mike's men had dropped a jailer. She just wished she could have put a bullet or two into the scum as well.

She and her partner had just pulled six more from another suite and were headed back down the hall toward the main room when Detective Sanders and a former Special Forces man either from Mike or Robin's people met them.

Detective Diana Sanders was tall, dark-haired, and as hard a cop as they came. But Sanders' eyes were round and Pickett could see she was breathing hard, more than likely from the run here and from this horror show she had found herself in.

"Just leave the door open after you have cleared a suite of rooms," Pickett said to her. "We won't duplicate that way. But make sure everyone is out in case someone is too afraid to move."

Sanders nodded, staring at the six people in their pajamas and bathrobes heading down the hall past her.

"Be careful," Pickett said to her as she followed the six survivors out toward the main living room and the tunnel door.

Less than a half minute later, she and Mike's man were headed back into the tunnel just as Sanders and her partner went through a suite door shouting Las Vegas Police."

She and her partner went to the next door in the seemingly endless hallway and had it open and through in less than thirty seconds.

And less than a minute later they were following Sander's group down the hall and toward safety.

Pickett and her partner had rescued 18 survivors of all this so far. They had less than 65 minutes left. There was no way they were going to get everyone before those bombs went off and brought all this down.

"Mike," Pickett said into her com link.

"Go ahead," Mike's calm voice came back.

"We're going to need to change up this plan a little to pick up speed. How about we clear a room and let the survivors just evacuate themselves back to the main room. We should be able to triple our speed."

Pickett noticed her partner nodding, but saying nothing.

Silence for a moment, then Mike said, "Seems like we have no choice."

There was a faint click.

"Listen up, people," Mike said. "Just clear the room, tell the survivors how to evacuate and then go to the next room. Jennings, I need you and Stevens in that big main room directing traffic out into the drainage tunnel. Carlson, you are in the tunnel pointing the way to the exit."

Pickett heard a couple of clicks as she and her partner headed at a run back up the tunnel. That might just get a bunch more out. But it was clearly more dangerous.

But after seeing all this, she was hoping against hope they would find a jailer so she could give him what he deserved: A bullet where his heart should be.

# CHAPTER FORTY-TWO

*October 20th, 2016*
*Las Vegas, Nevada*

It was on the eighth suite Sarge and his partner had cleared that things turned worse, if that was possible. Until they went into that suite, Sarge would not have thought it could be worse.

And by that point they were under fifty minutes left.

They blew the lock and pushed it open and instantly Sarge knew something was wrong. The smell of death smacked him in the face like a hammer.

Mike's man ducked inside to the left, Sarge went in low to the right shouting "Las Vegas Police!"

Two people, one man, one woman came out of the dark at them. Both looked like they hadn't eaten in months and were nothing more than skin and bones. They were both naked from the waist up.

As they advanced, Sarge could see the knives in their hands. And both had a look of anger and hatred.

And insanity.

"Las Vegas police!" Sarge shouted.

Both of the people just growled and kept coming, knives held high.

"Stop! Now!" Sarge shouted.

Made no difference.

Sarge took the man coming at him with the knife raised and shot him twice.

Mike's man took down the woman the same way.

"We need to check the bedrooms and bathroom," the guy said.

Sarge only nodded and stepped around the insane couple and headed for the bedrooms.

Every room was a horror show. Blood everywhere, signs of fighting. Two bodies in their beds, clearly dead. Two more in the bathroom.

Sarge just felt himself go numb. He wasn't really seeing this. This wasn't possible.

He followed Mike's man out into the hallway and pulled the door closed.

Mike's man nodded and took out a marker and marked the door with a bright "x" that glowed in the dark. Then he wrote "Keep out!"

Sarge glanced at a couple of survivors going past him in the hallway. They looked fine.

"Mike," Sarge said. "You need to warn everyone that sometimes the survivors are dangerous as well."

"What happened?" Mike asked.

"We ran into a suite that two residents had clearly gone a little crazy and killed the others. We put them down when they attacked us. We closed the door and marked it."

Silence.

Then Mike said softly, "Jesus, sorry I asked."

Then he clicked on the com link to everyone and warned them of problems with survivors. "Stay alert, people."

Sarge took a deep breath, then nodded to his partner. "We got more to get out of here."

Thirty seconds later they were going through yet another door in this endless hallway of nightmares.

# CHAPTER FORTY-THREE

*October 20th, 2016*
*Las Vegas, Nevada*

"Clear the area!" Mike ordered.

"Shit, shit, shit," Pickett said to herself. They had just gone into a new suite and had two unable to walk.

"We have five minutes," Mike went on over the com link. "Get everyone out of that area and into the big tunnel. We're going to bring up the power in three minutes and try to defuse the bombs in four. Move it now, people. Now!"

Pickett swore again, then turned to two men who had been waiting for her orders and who had told her about the two women who couldn't walk. They were standing in one of the woman's bedroom.

"You two," Pickett said, "Pick her up between you and get going. We don't have time to wait for medical."

"Why?" one of them asked as they headed for the woman

across her bedroom. She had wide brown eyes and looked scared out of her mind.

"The sick bastards who did this to you planted explosives. We're going to try to defuse them in a few minutes."

Both men nodded and then, as gently as they could, picked up the woman. They clearly liked her and more than likely had lived with her for a very long time.

Back in the suite hallway Mike's man had the other woman over his shoulder like carrying a light backpack. The other two women in the suite were already headed for the doorway into the hall as others streamed past, all in pajamas and bathrobes.

"We got anyone sweeping up behind us?" Pickett asked.

Her partner nodded. "Mike's got it covered."

She nodded.

But she didn't want to think about all the doors they hadn't made it to. The hallways past them just seemed to go on and on and branched.

If these hallways blew, this would turn into the most extensive rescue operation in history. Since the suites didn't have bombs set in them, the people in the suites would last for a short time. But not that long. Especially in the dark.

She just hoped Mike and Will and their computer experts had found the right way to stop this.

There were so many people in the hallway headed back toward the main room that it felt like a busy subway corridor at rush hour. Six teams had been opening doors along this hallway and then just pointing the survivors in the right direction. So some of the people were crying as they walked, others just sort of staggering along.

A few were helping others who didn't seem to be able to walk.

"Four minutes," Mike's voice came in strong.

Pickett flat couldn't remember how far down the hall they had gone. But she knew it was a distance and the one door into the drainage tunnel would be a jamming point as well.

She glanced back at her partner, who was carrying the woman over his shoulder like it was a normal day. Behind him she could see a couple dozen more people and then one of Mike's people bringing up the back.

This just seemed impossible, that such a horrible nightmare could be allowed to go on for so long. And right under the streets of Las Vegas.

She hoped that the Chief had arrested everyone responsible for this tragedy. And if lucky, they would all get small cells that never saw the light of day for the rest of their lives.

And even more sadly, every one of these people now moving down this corridor in their bathrobes and pajamas had once come to Las Vegas for the happiest day of their lives, only to find themselves down here like this.

Pickett had no doubt that some of these people had been in here for years and years, just holding on, living under the knowledge that every single moment of their day was being watched.

Pickett shook her head and then helped a man in a gray robe who had slowed down and was shaking. Clearly he was about ready to collapse.

"We need to get out of here," she said to him, giving him a shoulder to lean on even though he was considerably taller than she was.

He nodded. "Getting out of here is all I have been thinking about for three years."

"It's happening now, finally," Pickett said. "Just keep moving."

He nodded, clearly looking around and seeing everyone around him for the first time.

"They did this to this many people besides the six of us?" he asked, standing up and shaking himself slightly, seeming to come back into his mind.

"Far, far more than the ones you can see," Pickett said. "Far more."

"Oh, shit," the guy said.

Then he moved to help another man who was starting to slow.

"Three minutes," Mike said in Pickett's ear.

Three very short minutes.

# CHAPTER FORTY-FOUR

*October 20th, 2016*
*Las Vegas, Nevada*

Sarge saw Pickett come out of a hallway one over from his. They had only two minutes and the lights should be coming up shortly.

The big living room was jammed with people as the tunnels came down trying to get through one doorway. Mike's men were helping people along as fast as they could, but it was going to be close.

Very close.

Behind him the last people they had gotten to made it out of the tunnel. Sarge had no idea how many they had rescued, but he knew it was far from everyone. The tunnel went on past the last door they had opened.

And he was sure that none of the other tunnels had reached the last people either.

Robin came out of a tunnel two over and moved to join Pickett.

"Lights coming up," Mike said.

There were so many lights in the big room from all of the police and Mike's men that when the lights did come up, it didn't seem that different.

But the lights down the hallways came on as well. Sarge didn't let himself look back. He didn't really want to think about how many people they had not gotten to.

The room was emptying quickly. Sarge moved over to Pickett and Robin. "You two all right?"

"I will be if we get a chance to get back down those tunnels for the rest of the survivors," Pickett said.

"I just want to wake up from this nightmare," Robin said.

Sarge nodded.

The people in the large living room were now down to the detectives and Mike's people.

"Let's get into the tunnel and away from this door," one of Mike's men said at the doorway.

They all moved quickly, and Sarge let Pickett and Robin go through ahead of him just as Mike said, "We're going to try to disarm the explosives in fifteen seconds. Get clear, people."

Sarge and Pickett and Robin headed to the right along the old drainage tunnel at a full run along with six or seven other detectives.

The last of Mike's men slammed the big metal door closed and followed them.

After about ten seconds, Sarge took Pickett's hand and the three of them crouched down, backs to the walls as Mike counted it down.

At one, Sarge knew he was holding his breath. He had no

idea that, if that many explosives went off, the drainage tunnel they were in would even hold up.

The silence in the old drainage tunnel was intense as Las Vegas detectives and former Special Forces soldiers just waited.

Slowest few seconds Sarge could ever remember.

No explosion.

After a couple seconds, Pickett squeezed Sarge's hand.

He still didn't let himself take a breath. It wasn't over yet and they all knew it.

"We think we got it," Mike said, "but hold safe positions until we get past the full two hours. Another twenty seconds."

Sarge could only imagine how much stress there was up there with Mike and Will and all the computer people trying to disarm these explosives. Especially since Will's wife was down here.

Mike again counted it down.

Sarge again held his breath. He just couldn't help it.

After a few seconds past the final count, Mike said, "We're clear. Get the rest of those poor people out of there. Follow the procedure we have been doing and stay on guard."

Robin and Pickett and Sarge stood as their former Special Forces team members joined them, seeming to just appear out of the faint light in the tunnel.

Sarge nodded to them and all six of them turned and started back toward the big metal door that led to the cavern of horrors. Around them dozens of other teams were doing the same, this time walking instead of double-timing it.

The ticking clock was shut off.

They had survivors to rescue.

# THE AFTERMATH

# CHAPTER FORTY-FIVE

*October 25th, 2016*
*Las Vegas, Nevada*

Five of the longest days that Pickett could remember followed that long night in the underground hell. It had been almost ten in the morning before the teams started at the far end of the tunnels and checked every room and every closet for anyone remaining.

They had covered the body of the one jailer they had shot as they went past that suite and found no one else alive.

They also marked where they had found bodies in suites. Clearly people who couldn't hang on long enough and had killed themselves or died just days or hours before rescue was to arrive.

Sarge and two others found survivors hiding in closets too afraid to show themselves. And medical had to come for a few others.

Pickett and Robin and Sarge had finally climbed the stairs

all the survivors had climbed to get up to the parking garage. There was no chance they were going to get Pickett's car out of the mass of tents and emergency vehicles set up there now, so Robin called Will and had him send someone to pick them up.

Pickett was fine with that. She wasn't sure she could have driven anyway. At that point all she really wanted was a long, hot shower and some breakfast and a bed.

As they had walked into the daylight to meet their ride, the warm morning air felt fantastic.

"I think I had forgotten what daylight felt like," Robin had said.

Pickett nodded.

Sarge said nothing.

"Imagine how all those poor souls held down there felt coming into the light," Robin had said, softly.

"We got them out," Sarge had said. "That's what matters at the moment."

Picket could only agree with that.

The long shower, a light breakfast, and a few hours sleep came four hours later after they reported in to the Chief.

About five in the evening, she and Sarge met and went to the Golden Nugget buffet for dinner, then they had headed to the large warehouse set up for survivors just a few blocks away.

The entire Cold Poker Gang had volunteered to help, talk with survivors, and get information. An entire computer center was set up to find relatives of the survivors. Mike's people and Will's people were all working full time to help the police on this.

And the FBI and Nevada State Police had been called in and were starting to bring in help as well.

Two of the women that Pickett had talked to had been in the same apartment for over six years. Sadly, both of their fiancés had found someone else and married during those six years.

Neither woman blamed the men, but Pickett had no doubt this was going to be difficult going home, if that was even going to be possible for many of the survivors.

On the third day they had learned that they had rescued over nine hundred missing persons from that hell in the ground.

Nine hundred people got to be reunited with the families. The largest missing persons case in history as far as they knew.

And the place where the dead had been buried had been found as well and was being worked on slowly to put closure on even more missing persons' cases.

On the fourth day the story had finally hit the papers, without any mention of the vast number of people being processed. The story was about how thirty-one people around Las Vegas had been arrested in connection to a massive kidnapping ring. Details would follow, but Pickett had been glad to see the mug shot of August LaPine, the owner of August Tux Shop on the front page of the paper.

The Chief had warned all the Cold Poker Gang members to not come back on the sixth day to help. That's when the press would be there. But over the three days Pickett had gotten to witness more reunions than she could ever imagine. All of them full of tears of happiness and disbelief.

Pickett was glad that now, for her and Sarge and Robin, it was over.

But it was a long ways from being over for all the survivors and all their families.

For them, the recovery was just starting.

# CHAPTER FORTY-SIX

*October 25th, 2016*
*Las Vegas, Nevada*

That night, for the first night in five days, he and Pickett found themselves alone in his apartment, sitting on his deck, sipping a white wine and staring out over the lights of the city.

Even with all the ugliness they had uncovered, he still loved the city spread out below him. Loved it more than he wanted to admit, actually.

And he knew for a fact he was in love with the wonderful woman sitting beside him.

"That was a great dinner," she said, holding up her wine glass in a toast. "Thanks."

"My pleasure," he said.

And it had been. They had stopped at the grocery store and bought a couple of steaks and some salad fixings and he had grilled steaks for them. It had turned out better than he had thought it would considering how tired and drained he felt.

"What are you thinking about?" she asked, "besides this fantastic view."

"Actually," he said, "wondering what we were going to do tomorrow, now that this case is over for us."

"I have no idea," she said, taking another sip of her wine. "But I do know what I would like to do tonight."

"And what might that be?" he asked.

"I'm thinking we go downstairs, take off all our clothes, crawl into that wonderful large shower of yours and then toddle off to bed together."

"Can I wash your back?" he asked, glancing over at her.

She smiled. "Please."

"Then I like that idea a great deal," he said, toasting her with his wine glass.

They sat for the next thirty minutes just sipping on their wine, mostly in silence, letting the cool night air and the wonderful view clear their minds of the last five days.

Then they headed for the shower and bed. They made love comfortably, not in a hurry, and she fell asleep in his arms just a moment before he dozed off as well.

Perfect.

And for the first night since going down into the tunnels, he didn't have a nightmare.

The next morning they ended up reading the papers over breakfast in the Golden Nugget Buffet. It seemed that the press was having a field day now and the national news led with the story.

Sarge felt very happy right now to be retired and out of it.

After a while Pickett put down her iPad and looked at Sarge. "No matter how ugly all that was, we saved a lot of people, didn't we?"

"We did," Sarge nodded.

"That feels wonderful," she said.

With that he could only agree. It did feel great, and he was going to stay focused on that instead of the nightmare they had seen and experienced underground.

"So how about we go rescue some more beings?" she asked, smiling at him.

"As long as I don't have to go underground," he said, knowing exactly what she meant.

"That I can promise," she said.

They walked leisurely back to the Ogden and took her car and headed out the old Boulder Highway.

Twenty minutes later they were standing in a large glassed-in room that held a number of cats and kittens in large cages while others ran loose. The cat shelter was clean and modern and the cats all looked happy and well-fed.

Almost in no time he found himself holding two ten-week-old orange kittens in his arms. Pickett had a black kitten in her arms from the same litter.

And he was smiling wider than he had smiled in a very long time.

The moment he had seen the two kittens he knew they had to come home with him.

Instant love at first sight.

And she had picked up the little black kitten first and hadn't put it down as well. There was no doubt the two of them had bonded instantly from the way the little kitten sort of cuddled on her arm and just looked around without fear.

"Don't you dare call those kittens Come and Go," she said, then laughed at how one of the kittens was climbing up his chest.

"Wouldn't think of it," he said, enjoying more than he

wanted to admit the two kittens in his arms. "What are you thinking of naming that little sweetie?"

She held up the tiny kitten in front of her and then smiled. "Looks to me like he's going to be a long hair, so how about Harry."

"Well, that settles it," he said, smiling at her. He pointed to one of the orange kittens. "This is Dick and this one is Tom. That way if we ever live together the cats will be Tom, Dick, and Harry."

"Not a chance," she said, shaking her head and looking slightly horrified.

"No chance we won't live together?" he asked, knowing that wasn't what she meant.

"No chance we're going to name these cats any of those names," she said. "Let's get them home and let them tell us what their names are."

"I like that idea," he said, moving toward the front of the shelter with the two kittens. "But for the moment can I call them Pete and Repeat?"

"No!" she said.

"Spoilsport," he said, laughing.

"That's not what you said this morning in the shower," she said and gave him the arched eyebrow look.

"Did I actually say anything intelligent in the shower?" he asked, glancing at her and her new black kitten.

She laughed. "I'm not telling. But I honestly don't know since I was a little preoccupied."

"That's their names," Sarge said, smiling at her and pretending to be excited as they reached the shelter's front counter. "One is Pre and one is Occupied."

"No!" she said, her voice stern, her face slightly red. "Just no."

Then she reached over and scratched the chin of one of the orange kittens. "Trust me, little one, I'll save you."

Sarge laughed. He liked the sound of that and the promise of the future that it meant.

A wonderful future with a beautiful woman and three really cute cats. Didn't get much better than that in his book. As long as he stayed in his penthouse condo far, far above any tunnels under the city.

# FREEZEOUT

## A COLD POKER GANG MYSTERY

## DEAN WESLEY SMITH

USA TODAY BESTSELLING AUTHOR

*The Cold Poker Gang Mysteries continue with the next book in the series,*
*Freezeout. Following is a sample chapter from that book.*

# PROLOGUE

*March 3rd, 2002*
*Las Vegas, Nevada*

Sandy Hunter kissed her husband Rich goodbye in the modern kitchen of their apartment four blocks from Las Vegas University campus. Everything seemed perfectly normal. The morning sun through the kitchen window promised a beautiful spring day and that evening they had date night planned, with a wonderful dinner at their favorite sushi place.

Sandy stood five-two on a good day and looked much taller because she always wore heels, slimming black slacks, and had her medium-length brown hair pulled up on the top of her head. At twenty-four, she was just finishing her second master's degree in business. She worked part time at a securities firm and to everyone around her she appeared to be happy.

She and Rich had many plans for the future.

Rich still had a year to go on his second master's in history and was working at the university. He hoped to eventually become a professor there after a number of years.

He was short at five-five and Sandy often looked taller, something he didn't mind in the slightest. Unlike her, he didn't much care about his height one way or another.

Sandy told Rich she would be home to change clothes before dinner, then went down the three flights of stairs and got into their new Toyota two-door.

Security cameras showed that she pulled out of the apartment complex parking lot, turning toward Las Vegas Boulevard. In normal traffic, it would take her fifteen minutes to get to her office off Charleston. The morning's traffic was normal, as far as the radio said.

She had a meeting in forty-five minutes and had told Rich she wanted to go early to prepare. She had told her co-worker the same thing and they planned on meeting over coffee and Danish rolls thirty minutes ahead of the meeting.

She never arrived at work.

Just before the meeting started her co-worker called Rich to see if Sandy was sick or had forgotten the meeting. Both Rich and the co-worker were instantly worried that Sandy had gotten into a wreck.

After three hours of waiting and calling hospitals and no word, Rich finally called the police. They could do nothing, but a friendly detective listened to Rich and believed him and then called Sandy's office to confirm. Clearly something had happened to Sandy, so the police put out a notice to watch for Sandy's car.

At seven in the evening, Sandy's car was found parked in the Bennington Hotel and Casino underground parking lot just off the Strip. The hotel security cam showed Sandy pulling into the lot seven minutes after she left home, locking her car, and walking calmly into the hotel.

She seemed to know where she was going and was in no hurry.

She went to an elevator, and got off on the eleventh floor. She used a key card she pulled from her small clutch purse to open the door to a room halfway down the hallway.

The room was reserved in the name of Rich Hunter, Sandy's husband, and paid for with his credit card.

Rich swore he knew nothing about it and a check of their financial records showed that was the only time such a charge had been made on either of their cards.

Sandy's behavior was very, very unusual, to say the least. Yet she seemed to be acting normally.

Almost as if she did this every day.

At two in the morning, when the police knocked on the hotel room door, no one answered and the room was empty.

The security cameras showed that no one had left that room after Sandy entered.

And no one had gone in ahead of her either.

The room had been reserved online.

Sandy had left no fingerprints in the room, but the prints from the previous couple who had stayed there were everywhere. Nothing had been wiped down or cleaned beyond the normal maid service.

There were no leads and her missing person's case went quickly cold, with only her husband trying to find out what happened to his wife.

No one had any idea why Sandy Hunter vanished.

Or how a person could simply vanish from a major Las Vegas hotel room without a trace.

# NEWSLETTER SIGN-UP

Be the first to know!

Just sign up for the Dean Wesley Smith newsletter, and keep up with the latest news, releases and so much more—even the occasional giveaway.

So, what are you waiting for? To sign up go to deanwesleysmith.com.

But wait! There's more. Sign up for the WMG Publishing newsletter, too, and get the latest news and releases from all of the WMG authors and lines, including Kristine Kathryn Rusch, Kristine Grayson, Kris Nelscott, *Smith's Monthly, Pulphouse Fiction Magazine* and so much more.

To sign up go to wmgpublishing.com.

# ABOUT THE AUTHOR

Considered one of the most prolific writers working in modern fiction, *USA Today* bestselling writer Dean Wesley Smith published almost two hundred novels in forty years, and hundreds and hundreds of short stories across many genres.

At the moment he produces novels in several major series, including the time travel Thunder Mountain novels set in the Old West, the galaxy-spanning Seeders Universe series, the urban fantasy Ghost of a Chance series, a superhero series starring Poker Boy, and a mystery series featuring the retired detectives of the Cold Poker Gang.

His monthly magazine, *Smith's Monthly*, which consists of only his own fiction, premiered in October 2013 and offers readers more than 70,000 words per issue, including a new and original novel every month.

During his career, Dean also wrote a couple dozen *Star Trek* novels, the only two original *Men in Black* novels, Spider-Man and X-Men novels, plus novels set in gaming and television worlds. Writing with his wife Kristine Kathryn Rusch under the name Kathryn Wesley, he wrote the novel for the NBC miniseries The Tenth Kingdom and other books for *Hallmark Hall of Fame* movies.

He wrote novels under dozens of pen names in the worlds of comic books and movies, including novelizations of almost a dozen films, from *The Final Fantasy* to *Steel* to *Rundown*.

Dean also worked as a fiction editor off and on, starting at Pulphouse Publishing, then at *VB Tech Journal*, then Pocket Books, and now at WMG Publishing, where he and Kristine Kathryn Rusch serve as series editors for the acclaimed *Fiction River* anthology series, which launched in 2013. In 2018, WMG Publishing Inc. launched the first issue of the reincarnated *Pulphouse Fiction Magazine*, with Dean reprising his role as editor.

For more information about Dean's books and ongoing projects, please visit his website at www.deanwesleysmith.com and sign up for his newsletter.